murder
doubles
back

Sullivan Investigations Mystery
Book 3

Evelyn David

cover photo © Deviney - Dreamstime.com

**ISBN-13: 978-0615804842
(Trace Evidence Press)**

ISBN-10: 0615804845

DEDICATION

From MEB – With love and deepest gratitude
to my husband John, who has always encouraged and
supported my dreams. You make the hard times easier and
the good times even better.

From Rhonda – To my family for believing I could do it
and for putting up with me while I tried.

.

ACKNOWLEDGMENTS

Many thanks to the many Evelyn David fans who have encouraged, supported, and when necessary, gave us a kick in the butt to finish this long awaited third book in the Sullivan Investigation Series. We appreciate that you have had faith in us, even when we had doubts. We're so grateful that you made us revisit our old friends, Mac, Rachel, Edgar, JJ, and of course, the adorable and adored Whiskey, the Irish wolfhound.
Please enjoy!

CHAPTER 1

He'd never forgotten his failure, even without the annual postcard reminder.

Mac Sullivan turned the card over and scanned the message. He recognized the scratchy handwriting. Over the past 10 years he'd received a similar card every December. They had arrived along with the holiday cards at the police station. But this year was different; the postcard was addressed care of Sullivan Investigations. Someone's address book had been updated.

The picture on the front of the card varied, seemingly random tourist locations – around the DC and Virginia area. No pattern other than all depicting famous visitor or vacation spots. The postmarks changed each year but all came from Virginia. This year's card featured the Smithsonian.

The mystery had come full circle–back to where it had all begun.

The message on the postcard this year was the same as it always was. Block printing. A simple question. "Where's Amanda Norman?"

Mac's first thought; his mental response to the sender was always, "Dead." The second was a warning to himself not to ever say that word aloud. Technically Amanda was only missing. The fourteen-year-old went on a class trip to the Smithsonian and didn't come home again. The foster family didn't believe the teen was a runaway. There was no ransom demand. No reports of sightings. No actual body was ever found. He was the first and, as far as he knew the last detective on the case. He hadn't solved it.

A decade later, the Amanda Norman disappearance was a cold case, but not a closed one. The United States Post Office and a very persistent pen pal saw to that. It was only two months after Amanda went missing that the postcards had started arriving.

Now that he was retired from the police force and had his own detective agency, he was thinking that maybe it was time to warm up the Norman case. His holiday plans had included some quality time with his…He wasn't sure what to call Rachel Brenner. His girlfriend? Significant other? Rachel worked for his best friend Jeff O'Herlihy. At Thanksgiving the O'Herlihy Funeral Home had burned to the ground. Jeff had kept Rachel busy the last month helping him set up shop in a leased building and file mountains of insurance claims, but even workaholic Jeff had arranged for his staff to have a couple of weeks off from the middle of December until after the New Year. Jeff had kept a skeleton staff to handle any funerals, but Rachel was for all intents and purposes, on paid vacation.

Mac had already canceled two dates with Rachel during her down time. He had a feeling that last-minute trip to visit a distant cousin was actually her raising the dating white flag in surrender. She was a little vague on the telephone about when she was returning.

Determined to make a real effort, Mac stepped up his game. He made dinner reservations for New Year's at what Jeff had assured him was the trendiest spot in DC. Meanwhile there were several cases he needed to wrap up and a security job at a government contractor's office that started in a week. His calendar was full.

The timing of the arrival of this latest postcard couldn't have been worse. His staff of two was on vacation. He had a payroll to meet and bills to pay. His concentration was needed on the work in front of him and not the mistakes of the past.

Still...he hesitated to bury the postcard in the file with the rest. After all these years, why was this one of the Smithsonian? Was there a special significance that this year's card depicted the place where Amanda had disappeared? Had something changed for the sender?

He must have asked that question aloud, since Whiskey, his Irish wolfhound sidekick, felt free to vocalize her opinion.

Mac glanced at the dog, who'd taken over the dark green futon in his office, then back to the postcard in his hand. "Yeah, this time is different. It's not just about keeping Amanda's case active. Someone wants to tell me something."

***

"What is this?"

Mac Sullivan followed the sound of his assistant's voice into the reception area. He'd telephoned her earlier, asking her to shorten her holiday by a day and come to the office.

Julianna Jarrett, aka JJ, leather motorcycle jacket half off, stared at her desk and the large package enclosed in shiny red wrapping paper. Her short black hair was spiked. Several teal colored streaks had been added since the last time Mac had seen her.

JJ frowned. "You got me another Christmas gift? You rethought the prepaid gas card and travel-sized socket set?"

Okay. So maybe he shouldn't have left his shopping until the last minute. The truck stop on the way back from the Trenton job hadn't offered a lot of choices. But still, at her age, he would have appreciated some free gas money. And who couldn't use a spare socket set? But obviously his choices weren't festive enough in JJ's eyes. Of course, he'd also given her an extra week's salary, but he hadn't wrapped that in a red bow either.

He cleared his throat. "Edgar dropped that off for you yesterday when he got back from Taos."

"Edgar?" JJ circled her desk, examining the package from a safe distance. "Did you check to see if it was ticking?"

Edgar Freed was the other member of Sullivan Investigations. Closer to eighty than seventy, the wily, scooter-riding, oxygen tank-toting senior had the makings of a good investigator if Mac could just keep him from fighting with JJ. Edgar and JJ did an excellent job of pointing out the other's flaws and unsuitability for continued employment at the agency, but Mac was sure at some point their prickly relationship would evolve to one of mutual tolerance, if not friendship. Okay, so he was a silly optimist at heart.

"Be nice. He said he asked you to go on that ski trip with him and his great-nephew."

"Skiing? He can't even walk. The old dude was going to let that Navy Seal strap him to some cart on skis and push him down the mountainside. If I wanted to watch someone get killed, I'd go down to Southwest after midnight. Lots cheaper. And I wouldn't need to buy a suitcase full of puffy new clothes to do it."

While JJ was talking, Whiskey walked over and stuck her nose to the box, nudging it a few inches closer to the edge of the desk.

"Just open it. Whiskey can't stand the suspense any longer."

"Right." JJ picked up the package. "Not heavy enough to be one of those fruit cakes the old ladies in his neighborhood keep leaving on his porch."

Whiskey whined her displeasure.

"Okay. Okay." JJ grabbed a pair of scissors from her desk and cut the tape on the wrapping paper, revealing a white department store box.

She opened the lid, exposing a black ski jacket with dark orange accents around the collar and cuffs. Edgar had also included a stack of colorful postcards of the Taos resort.

"Nice jacket." Mac smiled. "Looks expensive."

"Yeah." JJ lifted it out of the box. "It's a bribe. He keeps trying to set me up with his great-nephew. Like we have anything but guns in common."

"Guns?" Mac shook his head. "Don't tell me, I don't want to know."

"Fine. But someday soon we're going to have to talk about getting me a carry permit." JJ put the jacket back in the box. "Look at these postcards! That's just the latest batch. I should never have mentioned I collect postcards. You say something like that just in passing to an old person and pretty soon total strangers are sending you cards from all over. Unlike the old coot here, most know to mail them to me so I have the postmark."

Mac smiled. "Speaking of postcards, I've got a job for you and the geriatric ski bunny. We need to track down a missing person. When was the last time you toured the Smithsonian?"

***

It was hard to pinpoint exactly when there had been a change. But as he ate a bowl of Grape Nuts, chased by a cup of one-shot coffee, Jeff O'Herlihy finally knew that he had somehow pissed off his wife of more than 30 years.

It's not that he wasn't capable of fixing his own breakfast. It's just that in all their years of marriage, Kathleen, love of his life, had always gotten up with him, made him some hearty fare (healthier in the last few years), shared a pot of coffee with him, before kissing him goodbye for his day at work.

But since Thanksgiving, except for the family-style breakfasts when all the kids were home, he'd been eating a bowl of cereal by himself in those early morning hours.

It was nothing overt. She wasn't sniping at him, pointing out his slightly paunchy stomach ("love handles" is how he preferred to think of them), no, nothing like that. She was just ever so slightly detached. He thought about their conversation the previous night.

He'd come in late after meeting with the contractor who was rebuilding O'Herlihy's Funeral Home. His business had been torched a few weeks earlier by competitors.

"Kathleen my love, like I tell all my customers, the end is in sight."

It was his normal mortician humor, but it didn't even garner a small chuckle.

He kissed her, as he normally did, but he might as well have been kissing one of the corpses he'd recently embalmed.

He tried another tack. "Have you heard this one? Who's the loneliest guy at the Middle School Career Day?"

He paused for a beat. It was like a knock-knock joke, he needed a straight guy for the joke to work. When all he heard was crickets, he went ahead anyway.

"The undertaker. Nobody comes to his booth."

She just shook her head and motioned for him to sit down at the kitchen table. "The fish is a little dry, what with over-cooking it. I'll bring over the rest of the meal."

"Maybe we could have a glass of wine with this feast," he offered.

"No thanks. I'll get you a beer."

And then they ate in silence. It wasn't the quiet he minded so much; it was that it was an uneasy silence. Like when he'd ask a question and she'd answer it, but not continue the conversation any further. All polite and that wasn't his Kathleen.

After dinner, he asked her to come into the den. He wanted her opinion on the carpet samples the contractor had brought by.

"What do you think? I know we've always used deep maroon, but I'm thinking that a pattern that looks like an oriental-carpet would be dignified, less likely to show dirt, and be a little different."

She looked through the samples quickly. "Do you really think anyone is looking at the floor when mourning their loved one?"

Jeff was surprised. He thought she understood the rationale for decorating the public area of a funeral home. "It's an atmosphere I'm trying to create. The receiving rooms should feel like someone's living room, where you can welcome the people who have come to honor your loved one and offer you comfort."

Kathleen looked at the samples again. "And the insurance is going to cover all this?"

"Well, not quite, but I think it's a good investment to buy a better carpet. It will last longer."

"Hmmm." She put the carpet squares down. "Whatever you think best."

And then she sat down on the couch and picked up her book. She read, he watched a little basketball on TV, and then they went to bed.

This brought him back to his cold bowl of cereal. He took another sip of his now tepid coffee. Maybe it was just post-Holiday blahs. The kids had all gone back to their own lives. Sean was visiting his sister in Boston. Maybe what they needed was something to spice things up. He could think of something.

Jeff took his bowl over to the sink and dumped the contents. Yes, he'd think of something. Turning on the garbage disposal, he grinned and reassured himself that if there was one thing he knew, it was how to be the life of the party, even if his audience was usually stone cold. Kathleen wasn't going to know what hit her.

EVELYN DAVID

Chapter 2

"Think we'll be done with this case by New Year's Eve?"

Mac glanced over at the old man driving the van. "I can't tell from your tone what answer you'd prefer. Got a hot date you don't want to keep?"

Edgar Freed chuckled. "You'd think the scooterchair would keep the quilting league ladies away, but I guess my natural charm is just too powerful. I accidentally accepted three invitations for dinner that night. A murder case is just the 'get out of jail' card I need."

"Natural charm my–"

"JJ!" Mac checked his watch, then his assistant who was on the back seat. "Please concentrate on that case file I gave you. I need you up–to-speed fast. We don't have the whole police file yet, just my personal notes, newspaper clippings and some copies of witness statements. And Edgar, until we know otherwise, this is a missing person case, not a murder."

"All this information needs to be converted to an electronic file so I can read it on my laptop," JJ complained. "Some of the newspaper clippings are falling apart."

"I didn't have any trouble reading it," Edgar said. "Computers aren't necessary for everything." He cleared his throat. "Mac, you have to admit that Norman girl has been gone a long time. Odds are–
"

"Yeah." Mac settled back in his seat. "I know what the odds are."

Mac and his partner Lyle Harvey had gotten the call around 1 p.m. on a blustery October day. They had just finished lunch, the highlight of an uneventful first half of a twelve-hour shift. At first, they had both believed the teenager had just gone wandering among the various buildings comprising the Smithsonian. First-time visitors were usually unaware that the Smithsonian wasn't just one museum but a collection of buildings. It wasn't unusual for even adults to get separated from their party.

He took a deep breath as the memories flooded back. The scene had not been secured. Evidence could have been lost. Even at the time he'd known that the search for Amanda Norman had been bungled. Against his protests, old Lyle, the senior detective in their partnership, had let the busload of teens and chaperones leave before everyone had been questioned.

"The witness statements are a waste of time. Didn't Amanda have any friends on the trip? Most of these are from kids who claimed not to know much about her."

JJ's question brought him back to the present.

"We didn't find any," Mac answered. "Amanda seemed to be a loner."

"This is a handicap spot," JJ complained as Edgar parked the van.

"I know it's barely noticeable, but I fit that description." Edgar looked at the young woman in his rearview mirror. "That's the reason I can usually find a parking place in this town. Why else do you think the boss had me drive?"

JJ grimaced. "Probably because my ride is in the shop and all Jeff O'Herlihy has in his fleet this week is a neon green Honda with a bad transmission."

"Enough, you two." Mac pulled the latest postcard from his jacket pocket and handed it to the old man. "Edgar, your mission is to find out everything you can about this postcard. Check out the gift shop or wherever they're selling this stuff."

Edgar nodded. "Wild goose chase. You can probably buy this postcard at almost any drugstore in town."

"Still, we have to start somewhere. Maybe this is a new postcard, just released for sale. This mystery started here; maybe my pen pal wants it to end here." Mac shook his head. He knew it was unlikely that canvassing the museum stores would produce anything, but it had to be done.

He turned to face JJ. "You and I are going to walk the crime scene and see if there is anyone still working here that recalls the incident. I'm hoping someone might dredge up something they didn't tell the police before. Remember being a detective ain't glamorous. It's 99 percent grunt work, one percent luck."

JJ sighed. "Right, I know. You've said it a hundred times, your job is to be lucky and Edgar and I are supposed to handle the grunt parts."

Mac grinned. "Now you've got it. Let's go."

***

Mac and JJ walked to the Air and Space Museum on Independence Avenue at 6th Street, SW. It was where Amanda Norman's class trip had been held. The enormous glass and concrete building was part of the Smithsonian Museum complex and housed the Wright brothers' plane, as well as the Apollo 11 command module. There were 23 galleries with hundreds of exhibits, exploring all facets of flight. Easy, too easy, for a teen to get lost, leave, or be abducted. Mac had no clue which applied to Amanda.

"JJ, you have her photo? There's a couple in the file."

She searched and handed Mac a 5x7 school photograph of Amanda Norman.

Mac sighed. Glancing at the photo, he remembered his frustration at getting a good likeness of Amanda. The photo in his hand had been ordered from the company that had taken the student photos at Eastern High School, a month before Amanda's disappearance. Apparently no one in Amanda's household had cared enough to buy any of the school photos. The foster parents certainly hadn't produced any others when asked.

Even with him pushing, the photography studio had taken weeks to track down the proofs, and by then the public's interest in the teen's disappearance had waned. He'd always wondered if he'd had a current photo during those early days, would he have found a witness or at least gotten a lead?

The case photo Social Services had in their file had been so old that using it had probably done more harm than good. Girls change a lot from ten to fourteen.

"How come nobody noticed the kid was gone?" JJ asked as she stared at the airplane that Charles Lindbergh had piloted on the first solo trans-Atlantic flight.

"Apparently she was new to the school. Hadn't made any friends. Teachers and chaperones barely remembered her." Mac looked at the school photo of the young girl, skinny, almost painfully thin, face void of expression, eyes hidden behind a pair of cheap framed glasses with thick lenses, blonde hair in a shapeless ponytail down her back. The too-big clothes were clean but worn. If she could have disappeared in a photo, Amanda would have.

Mac put the photo in his jacket pocket. "Amanda Norman had been in and out of foster care for most of her life. Nobody noticed her absence until she wasn't there to get on the bus."

JJ shrugged. "So she was just another kid dumped in the foster care system, with no one to give a damn about her. I'm surprised anyone spent any amount of time looking for her."

"I looked," Mac said, wondering again if he'd done enough. Obviously not, or he'd have found some trace of her. "Believe me, I looked."

JJ nodded. "I'm sure you did your best."

They walked over to another exhibit. This one dealing with space flight.

"Are these the real thing?" JJ stared at the moon rocks in the case. "Cool."

"Hey," Mac touched JJ's elbow to get her attention. "Come over here. The teachers said that they divided the students into four groups. Amanda was in a group with 18 other students and two chaperones. The last time anyone could say that they definitely saw her was right here."

Mac and JJ were standing outside the Wright Food Court, next to the Lunar Exploration Vehicles.

"I remember one of the teachers said she had called to Amanda to keep up with the group," Mac commented.

"Where was she when the teacher saw her?"

Mac pointed to the café. "They had a menu board outside. The teacher, Joyce Ames, thought the girl was checking it out."

"Probably hungry," JJ surmised. "She looks hungry in that photograph."

"Hungry?" Mac pulled the photo from his pocket and took another look. "I didn't think about that. There was nothing in the Social Service file about abuse or neglect."

JJ shrugged. "I imagine not everything makes it into those files. So did she do as the teacher asked? Rejoin the group?"

"That's what Mrs. Ames said." Mac continued to look at the photo. "The teacher continued the mini-lesson on the history of flight and the group moved on to the IMAX theater down the hall. They watched a film."

JJ snorted. "And nobody knows for sure if Amanda actually went into the theater with the rest of the group?"

Mac sighed. "Yep. Next time anyone noticed that Amanda wasn't with them, was two hours later when they were doing a check-off of the students getting on the bus to go back to school."

"And you expect somebody now to remember a girl from ten years ago? A kid who could have blended into that wall over there?" JJ shook her head. "Not likely."

Mac agreed it was a long shot. It seemed Amanda Norman had made little to no impression on anyone. Even her foster mother said the girl barely spoke, just did her chores and read. That was one the thing the girl did seem to like. Reading. She always had a book in her hand. To quote her foster father, "The girl was no trouble at all until she disappeared."

He made a mental note to interview the foster parents again if they were still alive.

"No point in talking to the food court servers," JJ pointed across the room. "All of them are in their early 20s. They wouldn't have been working here then."

"True. But still, this hasn't been a waste of time. Being here is refreshing my memories."

"Okay. You're the boss." JJ headed down the hall. "I'll be back. Got to find a...."

Mac nodded and leaned against the wall. Despite what he told JJ, he wasn't sure he was doing the right thing spending time on this old case. The detective agency was barely on its feet. Sullivan

Investigations was surviving on a month-to-month basis. He had enough to meet December's payroll but he wasn't sure about January's. And here he was using precious time reopening the Amanda Norman case that he could have spent on a paying client. Sure, the postcard had spooked him, but despite the sender's opinion, it wasn't his job to find Amanda Norman anymore. His job was to find answers for people who were willing to pay for his services.

He glanced back down the hall at the IMAX theater. Crowds were waiting to go in. Had Amanda watched the film and then left? Did she leave under duress? He shook his head. He had to stop worrying about a kid he'd never met. One who was probably long dead.

"Excuse me."

Mac was startled out of his thoughts by a janitor setting up some yellow safety cones.

"Sorry to bother you Mister, but a little boy threw up about fifteen minutes ago right where you're standing. Gave it a quick cleanup, but I want to sanitize it before the lunch crowd."

Mac hustled out of the way, and then looked back. The man was about 70 years old. He might be his best hope.

"Sir, could I bother you for a minute?" Mac moved next to the man's cleaning cart.

The janitor arranged the last safety cone and joined him.

"Were you working here 10 years ago?"

The old man nodded. "Been here close to 30 years. Lots of changes."

Mac reached into his pocket and took out Amanda Norman's school photo. "Do you remember this girl? Do you recognize her? Would have been ten years ago. Went missing after a school trip."

"I've seen a lot of kids over the years." The man took the photo and looked carefully. "Not sure. Maybe. This was the one, the kid the police searched for? The missing kid that was in the newspapers back then? I might have seen her."

Mac was surprised. When he'd canvassed the museum staff years earlier, nobody remembered seeing Amanda. He wondered if the janitor was mixing up the newspaper stories with his memories.

"Where did you see her? Was she alone?"

"I'm probably wrong." The janitor handed the photo back. "It was a long time ago. I can't be sure after all these years."

"This is important. Tell me what you remember. Did you see her or not?" Mac could scarcely believe his luck finding this guy.

"Yes, well maybe. At the time I didn't believe so, and that's what I told the cops who asked me. But today, now that I think about it, she kind of reminds me of my granddaughter."

Mac was confused. "Your granddaughter. You think the photo looks like your grandchild?"

"Just the hair. Or maybe the lack of it." The old man carefully took the mop out of the bucket. "Marissa, that's my granddaughter, last week she cut off her beautiful long hair so she could donate it to a charity that makes wigs for kids with cancer. She looks so different now. I almost didn't recognize her the first time I saw her after the haircut. Same with this girl."

"Explain it to me," Mac urged, not connecting the dots yet.

The older man continued cleaning the floor. "I'm probably wrong."

"Please, your granddaughter's haircut reminded you of...."

"The girl that went missing. Amanda something."

Mac nodded. "Amanda Norman."

"When the cops showed me that picture years ago, I was sure I hadn't seen anyone that looked like that. But the kid in the photo has long hair, like my granddaughter did."

The janitor put the mop back in the water. "There was a girl. In all the fuss afterward, I completely forgot about her. She was a skinny kid with ugly glasses who had short, kind of ragged looking hair. I felt sorry for her. That was one bad haircut."

"And she looked like this girl?" Mac held out the photo again.

"I think so. The face was similar." The janitor nodded. "Maybe she cut off her hair. Or maybe there were two girls and I'm just misremembering."

Mac thought a moment. "So you think you might have seen a girl that looked like the one in this picture, but she had short hair?"

"Yeah, maybe. She was coming out of the ladies' room, just as I was about to close it up for cleaning. She walked down the hall toward the exit."

"Was she alone?"

The old man nodded.

"Did you see any hair when you cleaned the bathroom?"

"No, course she could have flushed it down the toilet. And before you ask, I didn't spend any time sorting through the trash. The police had access to our trash bins, but I'm not sure they went through them. After a week or so, they said we could let the service haul it off like normal."

Mac didn't remember the trash issue. He'd have to check the police file and see if they'd had some uniforms search it. "What time did you see her?"

The old man thought a moment. "Back then, we cleaned the first floor bathrooms around 1:30, after the lunch crowd."

That was about two hours after Amanda had last been seen and an hour before anyone noticed she was gone.

The janitor checked his watch. "I'd like to help you, but I've got to get this floor mopped so if you don't mind...."

Mac moved out of the way. "Thanks again. If you think of anything else, give me a call." He handed him his business card.

"Funny, last week I would have sworn I never saw her." The janitor tucked the card into his pocket and started swabbing another area of the floor. "If Marissa hadn't cut her hair for that charity thing, it never would have occurred to me that was the same girl. Strange how memory works and the old stuff gets jarred loose."

"Thanks." Mac saw JJ coming back down the hall and walked to meet her. He wondered if there was something else he'd forgotten about the case. He wondered if there was something that would trigger a memory for him too.

After talking to the janitor Mac had to question whether Amanda Norman had been abducted or if she had just walked away.

If so, was she still alive?

***

"You called it, Mac. It's new," Edgar said, meeting them at the van. "The postcard is brand new. Limited holiday edition! Been on sale here about three weeks. The sales lady is going to check for me, but she doesn't think it's available anywhere else. At least not yet."

"That's good news." Mac smiled and leaned against the van. "So my pen pal probably purchased the postcard here. And he or she did it recently."

Edgar nodded. "Or had someone purchase it for them."

"Hey, can we get inside the van and talk about it?" JJ asked. "It's freezing out here."

"Just hold your horses," Edgar said, tossing JJ a plastic bag with the Smithsonian gift store logo on the side and his keys. "Help me get this scooter on the lift and we'll get out of here. I'm anxious to get us headed back before rush hour."

JJ shoved the bag into Mac's hands and used the remote on Edgar's keychain to unlock the van.

"Traffic in this town is getting worse every year. And if that's not enough, every vehicle you see is a black SUV," Edgar complained as they got underway. "Check out any parking lot, I bet three quarters of them are black Jeeps or Blazers. Politicians, drug pushers, soccer moms, all want the same ride. Look behind us. Right now there are at least three of them black SUVs following us. And that many or more in front."

"Maybe you should have bought one instead of this van, Edgar," JJ joked. "If you wanted to blend in, that is."

"I have never aspired to blend in anywhere," Edgar exclaimed. "I want people to see me coming and get the hell out of the way."

Mac chuckled. "I'm sure the other drivers try. For now maybe you should just pick a lane and stay in it. We're not in that big a hurry."

***

They were almost to the office before Edgar revealed what else he'd found.

"There are security cameras almost everywhere in the Smithsonian. I filed a request to get digital copies of the video from the gift store for the timeframe from when the postcards went on sale and the postmark date on your card. We should know something in a day or too. I gave them your Lieutenant friend's name and kind of implied he was interested in seeing them. You might want to give him a heads up."

Mac nodded. "Good work. I'm going to the police station in the morning to see about getting a copy of the complete case file. I'll mention the security video. But do you know how many of those postcards were sold? How many people are we going to see on those tapes? The video might not be much help."

"Never know. I'd never bet against your luck," Edgar said. "Besides, your pen pal seems to know you. Maybe you'll recognize him or her. The card was on a special display rack by itself. We just have to focus on that one location. See who picks up a card."

Mac glanced at JJ in the backseat. "You've been awfully quiet. What's on your mind?"

"I was just thinking." JJ leaned forward. "You were right about going to the Smithsonian and returning to the scene of the crime so to speak. But this field trip really pointed out the problems with investigating a cold case. A lot of years have gone by since the kid disappeared. Witnesses' memories aren't reliable, if you can even find witnesses. Are you sure you want to spend time on this? We have that big job starting soon and we've got a standing offer to provide Mall security during the next month. Easy money. This job isn't going to pull in any income, right?"

"Sometimes it's not about the money." He sighed. Not about the money. Right. Thoughts like that were why he lived paycheck-to-paycheck. "We'll manage, JJ. Maybe do some small side cases concurrently. Hell, if I have to, I'll bite the bullet and take a couple of surveillance jobs for Jerry Lazlo."

"The divorce attorney? You'll need to spend money for a new camera with a zoom lens!" JJ laughed. "How many times have you told me Sullivan Investigations doesn't do that kind of work?"

Mac chuckled and turned on the radio. Christmas music filled the van. "Let's just hope it doesn't come to that. I hate dealing with cheating spouses almost as much as I hate doing mall security."

"If I get a vote, I vote 'no' on mall security. Heck, old cases don't scare me," Edgar said. "This Norman girl disappearance is certainly more interesting than dressing up in a smelly elf costume and dealing with shoplifters. She was a foster kid. I suggest we try to get some more information from Social Services about Amanda Norman. How much of that will be in the police file, do you think? I mean, what do you really know about the kid? Where did she come from?"

"I don't remember what I knew back then," Mac admitted. "JJ, tomorrow you do some public record searches. Edgar, you check out the newspaper morgue. I was too deep into the investigation at the time to notice what the reporters were saying about it. See if some reporters had facts the police didn't. Meanwhile, I'll make some calls. We'll find out everything there was to know about Amanda Norman."

Chapter 3

"What's that?"

The desk sergeant was new and from the expression on his face, Mac gathered he had never seen an Irish wolfhound before.

Mac glanced down at Whiskey. The Irish wolfhound was attached to the end of a long thin leather leash. It was questionable who was leading whom.

"My service dog," Mac responded, not looking for a fight with the cop. He also didn't have the time or patience for a long explanation. He'd already had an extensive discussion with Whiskey about why she should wait for him in the car. She'd made her displeasure known to everyone within earshot after he'd naively attempted to execute his unilateral decision.

"You sure that's a dog? Looks like a small horse to me."

Whiskey made a sound that a casual observer would have taken for "Huh."

The desk sergeant narrowed his eyes. "Did she just...."

Whiskey stood up on her hind legs, resting her front two on the wooden countertop. She stared at the pudgy uniformed officer as though inspecting him for signs of intelligence and finding him wanting.

He blinked first.

"Who did you say you needed to see?"

"Lieutenant Greeley, Homicide."

"I'll buzz you both through."

***

Lieutenant James Greeley had been Mac's boss for the last ten years he'd been a detective with the DC police. Jim Greeley was a tall black man of few words and little patience for fools. He fancied designer suits, cowboy boots, and expensive cigars. Now that the police department had gone smoke-free, the cigars remained unlit. Looking at him, sitting behind his desk, feet propped up, and cigar dangling from his mouth, Mac was almost certain the man hadn't changed one whit in all the time he'd known him.

Whiskey pulled free and walked over to accept the Lieutenant's admiration and a scratch behind her ears.

"So what do you want?" Greeley asked. "I'm busy."

"I see that." Mac pointed towards the visitor chair. "Can I sit?"

"Go ahead." Greeley pulled out an ornate pocket watch and flipped it open. "Just don't get comfortable. I've got a meeting with the brass in ten minutes to talk budget."

"So I should dispense with the usual pleasantries?"

Greeley nodded. "Consider them said. Thanks for the early Christmas gift by the way. This one I'll actually use."

"I remembered what you told me would happen the next time I sent you a fruitcake. Actually I should probably confess...that fruitcake was one of about twenty that Edgar brought to the office. The old ladies in his neighborhood still keep him, and as a result, us, well-supplied." Mac chuckled. "But since I'm fond of the particular body part that you threatened, this year I just sent over liquor. JJ suggested we reserve the fruitcakes for clients who hadn't paid their bills."

"Well one fruitcake in a lifetime is more than enough for me. I still use last year's for target practice. Remarkable staying power." Greeley shifted his feet to the floor. "You're here for a reason. Time's wasting. Get to it."

"I've got a new case. Actually a cold case. One of my old ones. I need a copy of the file and some security video from a gift shop at the Smithsonian. They'll give it to me if you sign off on my request."

"Smithsonian? Some kind of robbery? Do you have a case number?"

"Robbery, no. Case number, yes" Mac handed over the information he'd committed to memory a decade earlier.

"That is an old number. You and Lyle worked this? Give me the headline." Greeley glanced up from the note Mac had given him.

"Missing teenager. She was on a school trip to the Smithsonian."

Greeley nodded. "Oh, yeah. Your annual postcard case. I remember. Kid went missing the first year I made lieutenant. Did you get another postcard?"

Mac nodded. "Came yesterday to my office. So somebody knows I retired from the Force. Local postmark. Postcard was purchased from the Smithsonian gift shop in the last couple of weeks. I'm going to spend a few days checking it out. Can't hurt. "

"I'm not so sure about that." Greeley gave him a sharp look. "These old cases can eat you up inside if you let them. Sometimes you just have to let a case go. We all have them. Odds are you're going to come up empty-handed again."

Mac shrugged. "She was just a kid, Jim. It's been ten years. A fresh look at the file might turn up something new. I've already got a few new leads to check out."

"Okay. It's your heartache." Greeley got to his feet. "The files are going to be in storage. Come back tomorrow. I'll have them brought up and left out at the front desk. And I'll give the gift shop, manager a call."

"Thanks." Mac stood, picking up Whiskey's leash. "I'll send JJ to pick up everything if you don't mind. Whiskey kind of freaked out your new guy."

***

"We're going to Le Provencal. I read that the mussels appetizer is to die for. The coq au vin is to die for. The chocolate mousse is to die for. I can see my obit already. She died from finally eating a fancy dinner."

Rachel Brenner waited for a reply to that important info. Her companion, furry and absorbed in cleaning her left paw, barely glanced up.

"You don't understand. I need to plan my outfit in advance. This is a big deal. The only meals Mac and I have had where a tablecloth has been involved have either been ones I've cooked or Luigi's Pizza which has permanently stained red-checked cloths."

Snickers, the pumpkin-colored furball, looked up and tilted her head to the side.

Rachel chuckled. She could guess what the cat was thinking. Snickers rarely had a tablecloth under her food and that omission didn't affect her appetite for Fancy Feasts.

"Okay. Point taken. But I still want to look nice. I don't know what to wear." Rachel stood in her closet, pushing one colorful top after another. "I think I might have overdone the quasi-gypsy look last year. I'd like something a little more sophisticated. It's New Year's Eve, you know."

Snickers still seemed unimpressed. She moved to her right paw. She kept her own wardrobe, orange fur, in impeccable condition.

"I don't know when was the last time I got dressed up for New Year's Eve. Heck, for a date with Mac Sullivan, I'm better off if I'm packing a Glock 9, than a silk scarf. I must sound like a schoolgirl getting ready for my first prom."

Snickers appeared to agree. Having finished her ablutions, the pudgy cat jumped down from the dresser. She glanced back at Rachel and meowed. The point was obvious to her owner. All that talk about food, especially fish food, had made the puffball hungry.

"In a minute. I've got to figure out what to wear."

Tail stuck in the air, the cat stalked out of the closet.

Rachel shrugged and went back to a review of her wardrobe. Maybe she'd buy herself something new.

She shook her head. "Get a grip. You just spent money you didn't have to go visit Mary; Sam's tuition is due; car insurance is due; and there's no guarantee that Jeff will be able to get his funeral home back open by the first of the year, so you could be out of a job." She paired some black dress slacks with a multi-colored tunic, and stepped back to gauge the effect.

"That should do it. And you know what," now talking to herself since her furry companion had abandoned her. "I'm not going to be practical. I'm going to wear Tina-Ho shoes."

She grabbed a pair of black stiletto heels from the top shelf and slipped them on. She teetered for a moment, and then struck a pose. The shoes were named for the skank who was currently enjoying the beaches of Turks and Caicos with Rachel's ex-husband.

"I couldn't do this every day, but I feel kind of powerful. 'I am woman, hear me roar'." She added a little hip wiggle to the song.

The doorbell interrupted the rest of the feminist anthem. Rachel slipped off her power heels, slid into her purple crocs, and headed downstairs.

She couldn't have been more surprised if she'd found Santa at her door.

"Aunt Ella, what are you doing here?"

"You going to leave your old Aunt outside in the cold or invite me in?"

Aunt Ella was her grandfather's younger sister. She'd left Thayer Farms, the family homestead in Warrenton, Virginia in her early 20s, vowing never to return. "Took me 22 years to get out of the country,

32

and I'm not going back," was Ella's oft-repeated philosophy. She actually did go back to Warrenton a couple times a year, to visit with old friends and join in some of the fox hunts, but when pressed, easily preferred a hotel room in any major city to the rundown farmhouse where Rachel had spent much of her childhood. The place Rachel still considered home.

As soon as the spry septuagenarian came in, Rachel hastily closed the door against the cold December wind.

"Seems like you might be getting a dusting of snow or more this week." Ella handed her niece a black cashmere coat, leather gloves, and silk scarf. "The cold goes right through me these days. I don't know how you put up with it."

Rachel hid a smile. This was a common complaint from her Great Aunt who now lived most of the year in Palm Springs, California.

"Weather guys think we might be in for a big storm." She hung up her Great Aunt's coat in the hall closet. "Let's go into the kitchen and visit. I'll make some tea."

"You got any of your Sugar Cookies? The ones you make with a hint of nutmeg?"

Rachel smiled. "I think I've got a few left. I sent most of them with Sam and his latest girlfriend. They're off skiing with her family."

Sam was Rachel's college-age son who was determined to spend as little time at home as possible. Once Christmas was over, he headed to Vermont with Laura or Lindsey; Rachel could barely keep up with her previously nerdy son's sudden social life.

Ella sat down at the worn oak table. It had been in Rachel's family for more than 75 years. She ran her fingers across the smooth patina of the old wood. "This feels familiar. Cookies and tea always tasted better at this table."

Ella gave her a rundown of her recent holiday cruise and by the time she'd reached port again, the tea was ready.

Rachel sat down across from her Aunt and poured from a blue crockery teapot that had belonged to Ella's mother.

"You really do love the old stuff, don't you? Always was a child that enjoyed living in the past." Ella added two lumps of sugar and a dollop of milk to her cup.

Rachel waved off the familiar conversation with her Aunt. The two women couldn't be more unalike, except for a complete devotion to each other. "I know, I know. Me and the crumbling antiques of yore. But tell me, what are you doing here? I thought you were going to be in California through at least April to avoid the," Rachel made air quotes, "the cold that goes right through you."

She paused, then looked at her Aunt again. "You okay? Is something wrong?"

Ella laughed. "You always were such a worrywart. I'm fine. Can't an old Great Aunt come to visit her favorite niece?"

Rachel reached over and grabbed her Aunt's hand. "Of course you can. I'm just surprised, that's all. Why didn't you let me know you were coming?"

Ella gave Rachel a quick pat, and then snuck another cookie. "I always was a sucker for these cookies. They're better than Martha's. I know you use her recipe, but…"

"It's the fresh nutmeg. Grams didn't put any in her cookies."

"Well, my sister-in-law was a stickler for following recipes down to the last teaspoon. I like that you're more adventurous in your cooking."

Ella paused. Rachel could feel herself getting the once-over by her sharp-eyed Aunt.

"You look different Rachel. After the divorce I was really worried about you, but you look…."

The old woman suddenly grinned from ear-to-ear. "You've got a new man in your life, don't you? Well, I'll be damned. Good for you."

Rachel couldn't figure out how her Aunt could still make her blush like an awkward teenager.

"Who is he? How did you meet him? Not someone from that funeral home you work at? I can't think of a more depressing place to work. Only thing worse than you dating a mortician would be you dating a cop. He's not a cop, is he?"

Rachel wished she'd put some bourbon in her tea. It would make the conversation a little easier. How to explain Mac Sullivan to her Aunt, to anyone for that matter.

"No. And don't get carried away. We've just started seeing each other. Would you like something more to eat? I have some leftover turkey and that green bean casserole you like."

She hoped that offering more food might distract her Aunt.

Ella waved her off. "I'm glad you're getting on with it. 'Bout time. You've been taking care of people your whole life. Well, now that I know you're doing so well, I don't have to worry anymore."

"No, of course not. You shouldn't be worrying about me anyway. I'm a grown woman. I'm fine."

Ella stood up. "Glad to hear it. I can see that for myself. It makes this decision so much easier. I'm just going to use your bathroom. I'll be back in a few minutes and we can catch up. You're not getting off that easy Missy. I want all the details about this new man."

Rachel thought a moment, then called after her Aunt who was heading up the stairs.

"What decision?"

She heard her Aunt's footfalls. They'd reached the second floor landing. "I'm selling Thayer Farm. We're both moving on with our lives."

Rachel sunk back into the old oak chair at the same oak table that had belonged to generations of Thayer families. Maybe only one of them was moving on. Suddenly, Rachel wanted nothing more than to put on the brakes and hang on to the past with both hands.

***

Mac dropped Whiskey off at the office before driving over to the ten-year-old address he'd found in his notes. The small brick house on 13th Street NE looked much the same as he remembered it–shabby up close, benignly neglected if you looked from a distance. As he parked he remembered something Edgar had said about black SUVs, that everyone had one in this town. Even in this lower-middleclass neighborhood, he saw one parked on the street and one driving past.

The doorbell on the house still didn't function, so he knocked.

"Yes?"

He didn't recognize the middle-aged woman in the faded dress who opened the door. She certainly wasn't one of the elderly Millers, Amanda Norman's former foster family.

"Hello, I'm trying to locate George and Diane Miller. They owned this house about ten years ago."

"I'm Louise Miller. They're my parents. They moved to Florida last year. Who did you say you were?"

Mac handed her one of his business cards. "I'm following up on a case I investigated for the DC police ten years ago. Concerned one of your parents' foster children that went missing."

"The only one that went missing!" The woman's expression hardened. "Unless you're here to tell them that she's been found, I don't want you bothering them again. They went through enough when Amanda disappeared. I'm not sure they ever completely recovered, but they have found some peace now."

"The police never blamed them for Amanda's disappearance," Mac said. "I know. I was one of the primary detectives on the case."

"You didn't have to blame them, they blamed themselves." She opened the door and gestured for him to come inside. "If you need to

37

talk to someone, talk to me. I can tell you everything they knew about Amanda and that school trip. I've heard it all, many times. I think they thought if they talked about it enough, at some point it would all make sense. It never did."

An hour and three cups of coffee later Mac left knowing a lot about the Millers, but very little new about Amanda Norman. The girl had been in the Miller home less than a year before she disappeared. The family never bonded with the child, although to hear Louise Miller tell it, they had tried. Amanda wouldn't let anyone get close.

"I had my own place, my own kids to worry about. But I saw her enough to get a feel for her when I visited. Tough little girl. Smart, but you'd never know it. Barely said three words a day. My mother told me that the only time Amanda would seem to warm up, even a little, is when they would bake together. The kid had a sweet tooth, but didn't weigh much more than one of those teacup dogs you see. My dad said she had a hollow leg, never could fill her up. I'm guessing she lived through some times of not knowing where her next meal was coming from."

One concrete thing Mac did walk away with besides an overload of caffeine was a large cardboard box of items that had belonged to Amanda. The couple had packed up the girl's things, expecting Social Services or the police to pick them up. No one ever did. Eventually the box made it to the attic, where Louise found it after her parents moved.

Locking the box in the trunk of his borrowed car, Mac was surprised when Louise Miller made another appearance.

"I don't know if it means anything, but my mother always regretted that they couldn't have taken in the other kid. See they weren't approved for more than one at a time. The house was too small."

Mac frowned. "What are you talking about? What other kid?"

"I thought you said you investigated Amanda's disappearance?" Louise stared at him. "How could you not have known about her brother?"

"No one ever mentioned a sibling," Mac said, mentally scrambling to process that information. The social worker hadn't said a word to him about Amanda having living blood relatives. "Social Services, your parents, no one saw fit to tell that to the police! I would have remembered. Damn it. Where is he? What can you tell me about him?"

"Hey, don't blame the messenger. I don't know any details," Louise answered. "And my parents didn't know about him when they first spoke to the police. It was months later that my mother accidentally saw a social worker's file about Amanda. There was some writing in the margin of one of the documents, a notation about a younger brother in the system. Mom said there was something wrong with the brother. He might have been in a special school. She wasn't ever too clear about that. I'm not sure she understood all of what she read. The boy was twelve, two years younger than Amanda. Looking back, Mom thought maybe the girl missed him.

She thought things might have turned out differently if the two had been kept together."

A lot of "what ifs" to think about. Mac drove back to his office wondering what else had been kept from the police. He was going to have to track down the child welfare officer who'd handled Amanda Norman's placement.

***

"Why are you selling the farm?"

Rachel kept her hands firmly around her teacup. She hoped her Aunt wouldn't notice the quiver in her voice. She was determined not to cry.

"Money, of course." Ella settled back into the chair.

Rachel almost dropped her teacup. She quickly placed it on the table, then put her hands beneath the tabletop, holding onto the seat of her chair in hopes she could stop the trembling. "Wha…What happened? I thought that Frank had set things up…You just took a cruise. I don't understand. Of course, you can live here with me. But what happened to your money?"

Frank Janowski, her Aunt's third husband, had been wealthy and set up a lifetime trust for Ella before his death, five years earlier. Comfortable enough from the divorce settlements from her first two marriages, her inheritance from Janowski had been substantial. With no children of her own, Ella had always been very generous to Rachel.

Ella snorted. "Don't be silly, Rachel. I've still got plenty of money. I have a once-in-a-lifetime opportunity to double my funds, but I need the cash from the sale of the farm to get in on this deal."

Rachel took a deep breath. So it wasn't because her Aunt was suddenly penniless. "What do your advisors say?"

Ella grimaced. "Bunch of old lawyer farts. Frank, God love him, set up the trust so I can't get to most of the principle. He was such an old fogey about money. Blue chip stocks, municipal bonds, all for a steady income. Took no chances. Hell, he passed on Microsoft."

"I'm afraid I still don't understand. You want to sell the farm to invest in a computer or software company?"

Ella snorted again. Rachel was beginning to feel like she was talking to Sam, her teenage son, who often seemed to have zero respect for her intelligence. Rachel dug deep for patience.

"What is it you want to invest in?"

Ella topped off her teacup. "It's not what, it's who."

Rachel just nodded, hoping her Aunt would get to the point.

"Martin Windsor. I assume you've heard of him?"

Rachel again felt like she was talking to Sam and being forced to admit that she had no clue about a popular rock band.

"I don't know Mark Windsor. Is he the head of a company?"

Ella rolled her eyes. So that's where Sam got that annoying habit.

"It's Martin, not Mark, Windsor and he runs the most successful hedge fund in America, if not the world."

"I thought that was Warren Buffett."

Ella waved her off. "Buffett is in the news all the time, but Martin Windsor is more discreet. I only got to meet him because I went to a cocktail party at Marnie Peabody's. You remember Marnie don't you?"

It was Rachel's turn to shrug.

"Doesn't matter. Marnie Peabody, or more accurately George Peabody, her husband, is a member of the lucky sperm club."

"Huh?" Rachel thought her head was going to spin right off her head.

"George Peabody inherited a boatload of money from his folks. He's not the sharpest knife in the drawer, but he's managed to keep most of the money intact. Of course, the way Marnie spends..."

Rachel held up her hand hoping to stop the train from going off the rails. "Ella, tell me about Mar...tin Windsor."

"Well, I went to Marnie's party and she introduced me to Martin. We talked about opera, thank God I listened to that Great Courses tape in the car. We talked about travel and I could hold my own there. Finally, I got up the nerve to ask him about investing in his fund. Unlike you, I did know who he was."

Rachel recognized a putdown when she heard one.

"And? He told you to sell your family farm?"

Ella threw up her hands in exasperation.

"Rachel, dear," Ella spoke slowly as if trying to explain calculus to a four-year-old. "Martin Windsor didn't tell me anything of the sort. He told me the minimum necessary to invest, and I think he was giving me a break because he was taking me to dinner the next night, but in any case, he told me how much was needed, I talked to my advisors, the old farts said "no," and I realized that they couldn't stop me from getting the money from the farm. They finally agreed to give me an advance on one year's income."

Rachel was confused. "What will you live on if you don't have your annual income?"

"Well, I could always stay with you until the money starts rolling in."

Then her Aunt burst into laughter. Rachel wasn't sure if she was laughing at the idea of living in a tiny house in Washington, DC, with her divorced niece, or just laughing at her divorced niece. In any either case, Rachel didn't feel much appreciated.

EVELYN DAVID

Chapter 4

"How you can drink this stuff?" Mac slid a large Gingerbread latte across his assistant's desk.

JJ waved him off, barely glancing away from the computer. "They're only available around the holidays. Reminds me of–"

"Of your childhood?" Mac laughed. "Would love to see pictures of you as a baby. Were you dressed in black diapers?"

"Yep, and my first shoes were hobnail boots, just like these." JJ struck out her leg and Mac stepped away from boots that looked like lethal weapons. "Now leave me alone unless you want to search the public records yourself. Not finding much. May need to file some Freedom of Information requests, but I still think you're wasting your time, and more importantly, my time."

Mac's cell phone rang.

"Sullivan."

He couldn't help but smile a little when he heard Rachel's voice. He listened, shaking his head as if she could see him.

"Never heard of him."

"I'll see what I can find."

He slipped the phone back in his pocket.

He approached his assistant's desk. "Get me what you can on a guy named Martin Windsor, I think he's got offices in New York, maybe LA"

JJ wrote down the name. "This another case we're not going to get paid for?"

"Just do it." Mac retreated into his office, where he found Edgar seated at his desk, the old man's scooter parked by the door. Edgar was moving his arthritic fingers across the keyboard of what looked like a new laptop computer.

"Didn't know you'd entered the computer age," Mac said, settling into a chair across from the senior citizen.

"Got to keep up or be left behind. Over the holidays my nephew helped me hop on the information super highway. Sure beats sitting on hard chairs in a dusty newspaper morgue." Edgar made a couple of notes on a legal pad, then looked up and cleared his throat. "I can search some more, but I don't think there's really more to find. The kid's disappearance barely made the papers for more than three days. Foster parents were in the clear almost immediately. Both had concrete alibis. To be honest, doesn't seem like anyone was really looking for her after the first couple of weeks. No pictures on a milk cartons or anything. No flyers. Just another kid who'd run away. Reporters moved on to the next headline; 'Mayor Flying High'."

"Yeah, literally." Mac sighed. He knew Edgar was right, but somebody was looking for Amanda. Somebody was still searching for her. Somebody who sent him postcards every year.

"You know what's funny?"

Mac looked up.

Edgar was flipping through the pages of his legal pad. "That house had a mess of trouble."

Mac was confused. "What house?"

Edgar waved his hand impatiently. "The house where the kid ran away from. Reports of it having been burglarized half a dozen times since she ran away. Maybe Amanda just wanted to get away from whatever had been going on there. Now the neighborhood's gotten, what do you call it, gentrified, you know lots of rich Yuppies coming in and fixing up those old homes, although her block is still sort of iffy. But back when Amanda was living there, lots of street crime. Maybe the kid got mixed up in something."

"What about the foster parents? Any criminal record pop up since then?"

Edgar shook his head. "No, like I said, they were clean. From what I can see, worked low paying civil service jobs until they retired. Took in a string of kids over the years. Nobody else ran away or got into trouble. Honored by Social Services when they moved to Florida a couple of years ago."

Mac thought a minute. "I'm almost positive Amanda didn't have a juvenile record. I checked it at the time. Of course there seems to be a lot of information that was withheld or misfiled for some reason. Like the fact Amanda had a brother. I ran Amanda's fingerprints through the system a few times after her disappearance. Never got a hit. I was expecting a body to turn up with a match. At the time I used the prints Social Services had on file for the kid.

With the way everything else turned out, could be those weren't right either. "

"You have a way to get another set of prints?"

Mac thought about the box in his car. "Yeah, maybe." He stood up. "I've got to run a couple of errands. Stop by Jeff's. Maybe try to find the social worker assigned to Amanda. Don't know if she's even still working for the department, but maybe somebody will still remember the kid. While I'm out, dig a little more. If nothing else shows up, see where we stand on the surveillance footage from the Smithsonian."

Edgar, already back checking the newspaper archives, waved him off.

Mac walked through to the outer office. JJ had a candy cane hanging out of the corner of her mouth, eyes focused on her computer screen.

"Anything?"

JJ shook her head. "I'd tell you if I had something. Still say this is a waste of time."

"You're getting paid for it," Mac responded.

"Yeah, right. Have you checked the account books lately?" She clicked off her computer. "I'm going to pick up some files from Jerry Laszo. He wants us to do some surveillance work and some Internet digging on a few of his divorce clients. Even if you're not ready to do the surveillance work, I can get started on the computer stuff. Somebody here has to bring in some money. Landlord is making noises about raising the rent. Then we'll be in real trouble."

"Hey, who's in charge around here?"

JJ narrowed her eyes. "I'll be back in an hour."

Guess there was no question about who was in charge. Mac watched her leave, only mildly annoyed. He was tempted to agree with her. It was a good thing that somebody was thinking of the bottom line. He sure wasn't. Shrugging on his coat, he was almost at the door, when he heard Edgar call out.

"Hey, wait a minute, wait a minute."

Mac could hear the old man slowly shuffling to the doorway. He waited.

Edgar finally appeared, breathless. "That house we were talking about?"

Mac nodded.

"There's been another break-in."

"What? I was just there yesterday. Talked to the daughter of the foster parents."

"Well good thing you got out of there when you did. Place was ransacked and…."

The old man started coughing.

Mac waited impatiently for Edgar to catch his breath. He offered him a bottle of water from the mini-fridge next to JJ's desk.

The old man drank it down greedily. When he got his voice back, he said, "She's dead."

Mac staggered backwards and slid into a chair. "Who's dead? Amanda? They found her body?"

"Nah. Woman in her late 40s, named Louise Miller. Daughter of Amanda's foster parents. She must have confronted the burglar and he killed her. Place was a mess. Took jewelry, cell phone, laptop, maybe other stuff."

Mac slid down into a chair. "How'd you–"

"Newspaper's website. Breaking news. I saw there was a murder on Capitol Hill. Glanced at the article and....Think there's any connection?"

Mac shrugged. "Seems kind of far-fetched. Been 10 years since Amanda went missing. Why break into the house now?"

Edgar took another swig of water. "I'm not much for coincidences."

"Me either, but sometimes a cigar is just a cigar...or a murder is just another random killing."

"You're the boss. You want me to keep looking?"

Mac was glad to know someone thought he was the boss. "Murdered. Hard to believe...."

"Well?"

Mac realized that Edgar was waiting for an answer to his earlier question. "Sure. Keep looking. See if there's a link. Find out if the cops have anything more on this latest break-in or any of the earlier ones. Give Pete Fiori a call. He's in Narcotics. Owes me a favor."

Mac levered himself out of the chair and headed out the door. He still didn't know what he was looking for or how to find it. He didn't even know why he was trying. The one thing he did know was that it wasn't going to be much of a happy new year for the Miller family. Daughter murdered; foster daughter still missing. Times like this, he was glad he wasn't a cop anymore; he'd always hated doing the death notifications.

***

Mac followed the sound of voices, down the long hallway of the new O'Herlihy Funeral Home. Jeff O'Herlihy, owner and chief undertaker, was his best friend, co-conspirator as a teenager in way too many pranks, and now the proud father of four children who he claimed were the cause of all the gray in his once carrot-colored hair.

After O'Herlihy's former establishment had burned to the ground a few weeks earlier, Jeff rented the space of what had been Franklin Funeral Home, shuttered when old man Franklin had been sent to his final reward.

As he neared what he assumed was a storeroom, Mac realized that he was actually hearing the sound of grunting, rather than any conversation. He looked in to find Jeff and Rachel shoving an over-sized brass casket onto a rolling dolly.

Mac laughed. "Expecting to send Jumbo the elephant out in style?"

Jeff pulled a worn handkerchief from his pocket to wipe the sweat from his brow. "Old man Morgan passed last night. He prepaid for his funeral about eight years ago when he was a size 58. I think he's been eating nonstop ever since."

Rachel slumped down on the floor. She ran her hands through her curls, also damp with sweat, and wiped her fingers on her jeans.

Mac gave Jeff a withering glance. "Where's your help? How about your teenage son? Somebody besides you, who's going to have a heart attack, and Rachel who couldn't wrangle a–"

He stopped when he caught a glimpse of the cold stares from the two of them.

Rachel began, icy disdain dripping from her words. "Thanks for your concern, Mr. Sullivan, but I'm quite capable of–"

She was interrupted by Jeff. "Death doesn't schedule itself, at least not usually. I gave my staff the day off and couldn't reach anyone. Sean is visiting his sister in Boston. Rachel kindly offered to help, and if you'd stop trying to run my business and pay more attention to your own, you wouldn't need to be over here every ten minutes asking for a favor."

"Sorry. Guilty as charged." Mac put up his hands to ward off the verbal assault. "I guess this isn't the time to ask to borrow a car? That neon green Honda stands out too much plus it backfires all the time. Makes Whiskey nervous. I need something inconspicuous. I hear SUVs are popular in this town this year. Got anything in a late model, preferably black?"

"Right. Visit a dealership if you want one of those." Jeff glared at Mac, and then waved him over. "Help me push this down the hall to the prep room. We might also need you to help place the body in the casket. Then we'll talk about you borrowing a car from my fine fleet of gently-used vehicles."

Mac was also drenched in sweat by the time they'd finished arranging Francis "Sonny" Morgan in his satin-lined coffin. He hated handling dead bodies. He didn't know how Jeff and Rachel did it all day long.

As he caught his breath Mac took one last look at the man in the expensive coffin. Rachel had prepared the body, artfully combing the man's four strands of hair over his bald pate, adding a little color to the bulging cheeks. Mac had to admit that "Sonny" probably looked better in death than he had in life.

They left the casket in the upstairs viewing room.

Jeff invited Rachel and Mac to his office for some "cold refreshments," but Rachel begged off.

"I'll talk to you later," she called as she was leaving. Mac wasn't sure if she was talking to him or Jeff.

The two men settled in comfortable chairs and popped open some beers.

Jeff took a long swig and started the negotiations. "No black, but I've got a dark blue Ford sedan you can borrow."

Mac groaned. "The eight-year-old one? Its transmission is shot too. How about your new Mercedes instead?"

"Not on your sainted mother's life."

"She always liked you." Mac smiled. "She treated you like a son."

"Not relevant to this conversation or my Mercedes."

"Come on Jeff, you don't have anything better than the Ford?"

"Beggars can't be choosers. Besides, it's fine going downhill. And it's very discreet. Unless you want to drive an old hearse, I've got nothing else available right now. The holiday rush hasn't started."

Mac sighed and held out his hand. Jeff flipped him a key ring.

"I'll leave the Honda keys on the front desk. I've got some stuff to unload from the trunk. Remind me who died and left you this treasure?" Mac asked as he pocketed the Ford keys.

"Irmegarde Schonenberg, a very nice old lady whose family couldn't afford much of a sendoff."

Mac grinned. "Probably wanted to send off her car too."

Jeff shrugged. "That too."

The two men sat comfortably in silence, sipping their beers.

Mac finished his brew and stood up to leave, but hesitated. "Hey, if I wanted to invest some money–"

Jeff sprayed his beer across the room "You what? You don't have enough money to buy a used car, and you want to invest in the stock market?"

Mac grinned. "Maybe I've been keeping a stash of money under my mattress and think it's now time to enter the world of high finance."

Jeff wiped up the beer with his dirty handkerchief, checked it, then unceremoniously dumped the cloth in the trash. "When you enter the market, Mr. Sullivan, remind me to avoid any of those stocks. They're bound to go bust immediately."

Mac sobered. "Seriously, I want to ask you about hedge funds. Rachel's aunt is about to sink a whole lot of dough in what looks to be perfectly respectable, but...."

Jeff looked at his old friend. "But something doesn't smell right."

Mac nodded. "I don't know squat about hedge funds or the stock market. I get a monthly check for my police pension, actually it's direct deposited into my bank account, and I've got no clue where the DC cops pension fund is invested."

Jeff shook his head. "Well that's stupid."

"Okay, okay, I'm no financial wizard like you. But have you ever heard of a guy named Martin Windsor?"

Jeff whistled. "Of course. He owns a very exclusive, very expensive investment firm. Why?"

"Wow." Mac sat back down. "You run in a tonier circle than I realized."

Jeff waved him off. "I know the guy's name. Follow him a little in some of the investment blogs I read. But I don't have the liquid assets to join his client list."

"Well, apparently, Rachel's aunt plans to sell the family farm, take an advance on her yearly income, and turn everything over to Windsor. The aunt is sure she'll make a killing, Rachel not so much. She asked me to look into the guy."

Jeff paused for a moment, and then spoke quietly. "If you believe everything you read, Windsor has a Midas touch. But my granddad used to say, 'If you can't use it, touch it, eat it, or drink it, don't buy it'."

Mac laughed. "Thanks for that homespun bit of wisdom, but what the hell does it mean?"

Jeff didn't crack a smile. "Look, I know you and just about everybody else thinks I'm a little crazy when I take a car in trade for a funeral."

Mac started to speak, but stopped when Jeff held up his hand.

"But I know what I'm doing. Sure sometimes I take the short end of the bargain, like the old Ford, but I'm making the choice because I knew Mrs. Schonenberg and I wanted her to have a funeral that would make her family proud. But I make those business decisions with full knowledge. Same with my portfolio. I'm not Martin Windsor and I don't get the kind of return on investment that he gets, but I do my homework, know what I'm buying, take calculated risks, and always, always want the company I'm investing in to be making something that I can touch. In other words, I don't take flyers on technology I don't understand."

"Do you think Windsor is legit?"

"Hard to say." Jeff stood up and waited for Mac to join him. "I've got to get home and eat some dinner before tonight's viewing. I'll help you move the stuff to the Ford."

The duo walked out to the parking lot and Mac got the box with Amanda Norman's possessions from the trunk of the Honda and handed Jeff the keys. "Thanks."

Jeff stopped before getting into his car. "Mac, I have absolutely no concrete reason to believe that Martin Windsor isn't exactly who he says he is, but...." Jeff sighed. "But, I don't. I've looked at his materials and his return on investment just doesn't make sense to me. Not that they'd be interested in what I have to say, but I got nothing to give to the Securities and Exchange Commission except my gut instinct. I'm pretty sure you remember what Sister Mary Margaret used to tell us."

Jeff looked at Mac who remembered exactly what the ancient nun who taught them fourth grade always intoned.

"If it seems too good to be true, it usually isn't," Mac said.

***

Rachel stood outside The Clarion apartment building on 20th Street, right off Kalorama Road. It was probably the oldest, grandest, and most exclusive residence in the District, much like The Dakota, the famed luxury apartment building in New York City. Built at the turn of the 20th century, The Clarion had 10 foot ceilings, crown moldings, heart of pine floors, Victorian-tiled fireplaces, and even still boasted of manned vintage elevators. It was rumored that the operators were as old as the lifts they rode. Jeff had sent Rachel to meet with Eugenia Morgan, widow of Sonny Morgan, the over-sized corpse that she and Jeff had just prepared for a final send-off.

Rachel straightened her silk scarf, gift of Aunt Ella, arranged her black raincoat, and wished her hair would behave. She had a hair appointment for a cut. Maybe she'd have a little color job. What had been a few strays gray hairs seemed to have suddenly mushroomed. Maybe she'd go blond, really shake things up.

A white-gloved doorman held open the door. She gave her name to the woman behind the gleaming mahogany desk.

"Mrs. Morgan is expecting you. Please take elevator 2 to the twelfth floor."

Rachel crossed the lobby, wishing her heels didn't clatter so much on the marble floors. She ran her hands through her dark curls, knowing the outcome wouldn't improve the situation. The elevator operator didn't say a word until they reached the top floor.

"To your right, Ma'am."

It appeared that the Morgan family apartment took up half the floor.

She had barely knocked when the door was opened by an elderly man in a dark gray suit.

"Mrs. Brenner?"

Rachel nodded.

He opened the door wide.

"Mrs. Morgan is waiting for you in the library. May I have your coat?"

Rachel wondered if she had wandered into a 1940s British film. She followed the gentleman through the living room into a paneled library, lined floor-to-ceiling with books. Eugenia Morgan, in her late 70s, was seated in a leather wing chair, holding a legal pad with a full list, from what Rachel could tell.

"Thank you Mrs. Brenner for coming to me. I know my husband already made most of the arrangements for the funeral, but I just want to be sure that...."

Rachel sat down on a side chair next to the elderly widow.

"I understand from Jeff that you've known the O'Herlihy family for many years."

Mrs. Morgan gave a tentative smile. "I've known Jeff O'Herlihy since he was swiping candy from the case in my father's grocery store. We've come a long way from those days on 11th Street."

"Then you know that he will handle this with the grace and dignity that you want for your husband. I promise you, just tell us what we can do to help you, and it's done."

The widow's smile widened. "I know. I worried that Sonny, my husband, you know he'd put on a little weight and maybe you wouldn't be able to...."

Rachel squeezed the widow's hand. "It was no problem at all. Jeff and I prepared your husband's body this morning. The casket and the viewing room are ready. I understand that you want visitation from 7 to 9 tonight, and then again an hour before the funeral tomorrow?"

Eugenia Morgan nodded.

Rachel leaned back and said with authority. "Now show me the rest of your list."

Forty-five minutes later, the widow was much relieved that between her husband's arrangements and the personal efforts of O'Herlihy Funeral Home, the final farewell for her late spouse would be handled as she hoped.

"Now if there's nothing more I can do to help you," Rachel rose.

"Forgive me. May I offer you some tea or coffee?"

"No thank you." Rachel paused and looked around the room, filled with books and family photos. "I love this room. I feel like I know you and your husband just by looking around."

"You're right. This is where we spent most of our time, reading, chatting, and I guess you can tell from my husband, eating. He had such a fondness for sweets. I could never deny him." The widow laughed.

Rachel looked out the window at the breathtaking view of the city. "Have you lived here long?"

"We moved in about 25 years ago, when we sold the big house in Chevy Chase. We wondered if we would be approved by the Co-op board. Sonny had taken over my father's grocery store and built a good business from that, but still, he was basically a grocer." Mrs. Morgan laughed again.

"Morgan Grocery Stores are out of this world. I love browsing the aisles. The prepared foods section is enough to make me never cook again," Rachel answered.

"Sonny always did have his finger on the pulse of what families needed. But still, Co-op boards demand to see all your financials before they let you buy. It was a grueling process even 25 years ago and nowadays, it's even more demanding. Sonny was on the board for The Clarion. Went to his last meeting a couple of weeks ago."

The elderly widow lowered her voice to a whisper. "You wouldn't believe who the board turned down. One of the biggest private hedge fund owners around, but according to my Sonny, the numbers just didn't add up. Other members of the board were more than ready to let this man buy the apartment–the other half of this floor. But my Sonny knows how to read a ledger and as he said, it was all smoke and mirrors. Lots of talk about millions of dollars, but when it came down to it, the man had barely $50,000 in his bank account. As my Daddy used to say, 'he's all hat and no cattle'."

The hairs on the back of Rachel's neck bristled.

"Forgive me, but are you talking about Martin Windsor?"

The old woman cheeks reddened. "Oh my, I've said too much. Please, you won't repeat anything I've said. The board's actions are confidential."

Rachel patted the woman's hand. "No, no. I promise you haven't revealed anything. I won't tell a soul."

"Sonny would kill me if he knew I'd been talking about..." She stopped and sniffed.

"Really. You know that anything you say to a funeral home employee is strictly confidential." Rachel said it with as much authority as she could muster. It wasn't true, but the widow needed the reassurance.

Just then the elderly butler appeared. "Mrs. Morgan, your daughter is on the line. I'll see Mrs. Brenner out if you're done."

***

It was healthy. He knew that. In fact, most of the meals he was eating lately were healthy.

Jeff O'Herlihy sighed. He glanced at his wife, taking broccoli spears from the microwave where she'd just steamed them. Little hope that there would be a cheese sauce on top. She brought the bowl to the table, along with another of some sort of grain, definitely not pasta or rice.

Kathleen was the same size she was when he'd married her, maybe even a little thinner.

He looked a little closer. Yes, definitely thinner.

"Are you okay?" He couldn't keep the worry out of his voice.

Kathleen helped herself to a piece of broiled fish and several spears of broccoli.

"Yes, of course. Why do you ask?"

"You look like…have you lost weight? Everything okay?"

Kathleen smiled. "I've lost a few pounds but I'm putting on muscle." She flexed her arm and he could see a tight bicep. "I've been spending a little extra time at the gym. Love this spinning class I'm taking."

"Spinning? Like Sleeping Beauty? Or was it Rapunzel?" He was confused.

Kathleen laughed. It was actually the first time he'd heard her laugh in weeks. He didn't care if he was making a fool of himself. Hearing her laugh was worth it.

"No, spinning like bike riding, only the bikes don't move. We listen to music and an instructor gives directions so we change the resistance settings so it's like we're going up hills. What a workout!"

He smiled at her. "So no wool is involved?"

She grinned. "No sheep are harmed in spinning classes."

"You don't need to lose any weight. You're perfect." Jeff knew he had a cheesy grin on his face, but didn't care.

"However, you, my love, do need to lose a few pounds." The sting was eased a little when Kathleen reached across the table to hold his hand.

"I'm not interested in riding a bike to nowhere." Try as he might, there was still a whine in his voice.

Kathleen squeezed his hand, which helped.

"I totally understand. But how about a bike trip in Napa? Cycling from vineyard to vineyard, but nothing too strenuous. Luxurious accommodations at little inns, gourmet meals and wine every night?"

He looked at his wife of more than 30 years and was struck by how she could still surprise him. Biking as a vacation? "How about a cruise, with all you can eat buffets?"

Kathleen slid her hand back across the table. "Cruises are nice. But this would be an adventure."

Jeff tried another tack. "I haven't been on a bike in more than 40 years. Don't think my knees would hold up. How about we rent a beach house for a week this summer? The kids could all come. Sun, sand—"

"Me doing laundry and fixing meals for seven days. Yep that's what I call a vacation."

"You used to love it when we'd rent a house at the shore."

Kathleen picked up her fork and stabbed a spear of broccoli. "I used to eat hot peppers with cream cheese, but now they just give me heartburn. I want an adventure and you just want the same old same old."

Jeff knew he was floundering. "How about instead of going to Ocean City, we go to Cape Cod?"

"A beach is a beach is a beach."

Kathleen took a final bite of her fish. Then picked up her plate and took it to the sink.

Jeff had lost his appetite along with the argument. He glanced at the clock. He needed to get back for the Morgan visitation. He brought his plate over and leaned in for a kiss. He got one, but he'd have just as well kissed the stationery bike that started all of this. Bikes don't move unless someone's pedaling, and Kathleen was standing stock still.

***

"Miz Brenner, hey there! Miz Brenner!"

Rachel turned to see her neighbor Edgar Freed on his electric scooterchair coming down the sidewalk.

"The FedEx man left a package at your front door, but I didn't want to take a chance that somebody might steal it, so I kept it for you." The old man was breathless after the ride and explanation.

Rachel took the square package.

"'Pears' to be from one of your friends down in the country," Edgar added.

Rachel was surprised he hadn't had the parcel x-rayed.

"Thanks Edgar." She looked at the expectant face of the old man.

"Would you like to come in for some tea?"

The grin answered her question. "You got any of those sugar cookies?"

Rachel smiled. "Already eaten the ones I gave you?"

Edgar levered off his scooter and hobbled along to the front door. "Didn't last but one night. My great nephew was visiting and he must have eaten a dozen all by himself."

Edgar's great nephew was a Navy Seal, so Rachel doubted he was the one gobbling up most of the cookies. But the old man was thin as a reed, so the calories couldn't hurt him.

"Come on back to the kitchen," Rachel called. "I'll put on the kettle. Here are the remains of the holiday baked goods." She put a plate of various baked treats on the old oak table. "Not much left. Sam took a big parcel with him when he went to visit his girlfriend."

Edgar slid into one of the oak chairs, just as the doorbell rang.

"Who could that be? Excuse me." Rachel headed back out to the front of the house.

"Make your old aunt a cup of tea?" Ella stood waiting on the doorstep.

"Sure. Come on in. Edgar, my neighbor, is here too."

Rachel found the old man happily munching on a decorated Santa Claus cookie, with the crumbs of an iced reindeer cookie on the napkin in front of him. She poured the hot water into the crockery teapot, added two teaspoons of loose Earl Grey tea leaves, filled the creamer and sugar bowl, and brought it all to the table. Ella had already helped herself to a homemade brownie.

"I gain ten pounds every time I visit you," Ella complained good-naturedly. "I'm going to be living at the gym when I get back to California."

Edgar eyed the remaining brownie and Rachel pushed it over to him. "Go ahead, I have more."

"I had lunch with Tom Hamilton today." Ella nibbled at her brownie.

"The realtor?" Rachel steeled herself. How long before her childhood home was sold?

"There's a problem."

Rachel forced herself not to smile. "Hmmmm. What kind of problem?"

"Apparently, Tom's buyer intended to use part of the land for one of those big box stores. Didn't tell me which one but it's the kind where you can buy a lifetime supply of tampons for like $3."

Edgar started to cough. Rachel hastily offered him some water. He drank it and started to calm down.

Ella ignored the glares from Edgar and kept talking. "Anyway, Warrenton had a referendum two years ago and overwhelmingly voted to ban any of those huge box stores from building in the area. Worried those kinds of establishments would be too much competition for local small businesses. Tom said that the box store corporate office might be willing to try and get approval, but we're talking months, if not years. I don't think Martin Windsor is going to wait if I can't get my money together within the next 30 days."

Rachel thought she'd just won the lottery. Maybe Thayer Farm would stay in the family. "So what will you do?"

Ella finished the brownie and reached for another. "This is a chance of a lifetime, but I don't want to have a fire sale on the farm."

Edgar cleared his throat, and then spoke firmly. "Why, land is the only thing in the world worth workin' for, worth fightin' for, worth dyin' for, because it's the only thing that lasts."

Rachel was as surprised as if her neighbor had just recited a Shakespearean sonnet. "Why Edgar. That's beautiful. My grandfather believed that."

Ella snorted. "Oh for goodness sakes, Rachel. That's from *Gone with the Wind*."

Edgar waved a gnarly finger at Ella. "Might be from a movie, but it don't mean it ain't true. You're fixing to sell your family land to invest in what exactly?"

Ella pushed Edgar's finger away from her face. "You wouldn't understand, but Martin Windsor is a brilliant investor. The returns on investments with his fund are double what I'm getting from my current advisors."

Rachel hesitated, then plunged ahead. "But how well do you really know Martin Windsor? I heard something today that sounds like he might be overstating his worth."

Ella laughed. "Trust me, Rachel. Martin couldn't keep up his lifestyle if he didn't have every penny of the more than $800 million the fund is worth. He's got homes in France, California, Florida, and he's buying a new place here in Washington."

"But what I heard...."

Ella waved her off. "It's all water under the bridge now. I don't have the minimum I need to invest. I just wanted to bring you up to date. I guess you're celebrating that, at least for the time being, I'm keeping the farm. But you can't be living in the past, Rachel. You've got to move on."

Rachel felt like a child being told she was too old to play with dolls, even if she still liked them.

"I don't think you know Miz Brenner as well as you think you do." Edgar stood up. "Why she dumped that sorry ass husband of hers and found herself a new man whose worthy of her. She works, has a kid going to a fancy college, ain't nothing off you if she loves the country life. Not for me, of course. I'm more a man about town, but Miz Brenner here seems to have her feet on the ground. I'd put my money on her judgment before I'd trust some man who takes money from old ladies to make himself richer."

Edgar tottered to the front door. "Thank you so much Miz Brenner. Always a pleasure to spend time with you."

Rachel hid a smile as her aunt fumed.

"Who is that old fool calling old?"

Chapter 5

The next day promised snow, and if the Tylenol he'd taken didn't kick in soon, a backache might have him stretched out on the floor of his office instead of working the Amanda Norman case. He had a dinner date with Rachel for later that night, but was considering canceling to focus on the long-missing teen. Some boyfriend he was.

"What do we know?" Mac Sullivan asked the question as Whiskey and he entered the office. He was carrying the old cardboard box of Amanda's belongings. Whiskey was toting a fresh Happy Meal, the paper bag dangling from her mouth. Judging from the frown on JJ's face as she walked towards him, Whiskey was the only one in a good mood.

"Not much," JJ answered. She pointed towards the other side of the office. "But we have a lot of reading to do. I've already been to the police department and picked up the Amanda Norman case files."

JJ had set up an erasable white board along with a worn folding table once used in an elementary school cafeteria. The board was blank. A clean slate, so to speak. The table was loaded. Sturdy and cheap, after eight hours of petrified chewing gum removal, the table was a real bargain. The contents of Amanda Norman's police file were spread out on it, organized in a manner that only JJ would understand. He saw at least ten separate, neatly stacked piles. He sat the cardboard box next to the last one.

"We have the digital files from the Smithsonian gift shop," JJ said. "I have them loaded on the laptop. There something like 140 hours of recordings. Do you want me to–"

Mac shook his head. "I'll start looking at them later. First let's go through the police files. I've got someone coming in at 11 am, so we need to get busy. Where's Edgar?"

"Beats me. He finished the newspaper search yesterday. That red folder is his research." JJ pointed to the first pile and the brightly colored folder on top. "He called and said he'd be a few hours late. Old fool said he had to see a man about a dog. What does that mean anyway? I know it has nothing to do with dogs."

"It's just...Never mind." He nodded towards the white board. "Let's start a timeline."

"The police call came in at–"

"No." Mac rolled a chair over to the table and eased down into it. He took some latex gloves from his pocket and a plastic baggie. Gloves on, he opened the cardboard box. "I don't want to repeat my first mistake. Let's start farther back. Make no assumptions. Write down Amanda's date of birth. We'll begin there."

***

"What do you mean, you don't have gas?"

"I prefer using injections. I've found they're more than adequate for most dental procedures."

"I'm not into pain," Edgar warned. "Let's just be clear here, you hurt me, I hurt you."

"Relax, Mr. Freed. I'm a professional. Open wide."

"Let's chat a minute first. I like to know who's putting their fingers in my mouth. Why are you opening an office in this crummy part of town? Just get out of prison or something?" Edgar had encountered a bad raisin in his morning bran and knocked a crown loose. His regular dentist had a four week wait list for appointments. This guy, Dr. Payne, took walk-ins. And with his office one flight up from Mac's, he was handy.

Edgar noted that the man was wearing an expensive suit that had seen better days, much like the man himself. Medium height and with a golfer's tan, the dentist's overly confident manner seemed more than the shabby surroundings would support for any length of time. Edgar figured the man was new to his apparently lower station in life.

"Mr. Freed. Please be assured that I have no criminal record. I'm fully credentialed. I'm just here starting over. Reconnecting with the basics in life. This area of town is affordable and I hoping in the future it will undergo a rebirth much like myself; a phoenix rising from the ashes."

"Bad divorce settlement?" Edgar guessed. "She clean you out?"

The fifty-something dentist sighed. "Everything I had and half of what I earn for the next five years. Speaking of which, I accept all major credit cards and insurance, but I give a 30% discount for cash."

***

"Write down the name, Hugo Alvira."

"Who was he?" JJ asked, facing the board, the black marker in her hand stilled.

"A foster parent, according to Social Services." Mac held up a thin folder that he'd added to the pile. It contained notes from his early morning telephone conversation with a helpful retired DHS worker. "He and his ailing wife Lisa, were foster parents number two. She had kidney problems. Amanda was in his care for three years–the longest she'd stayed anywhere. The brother was there too, before he was moved to a special school. Apparently Hugo supplemented his living with a steady series of home burglaries to help pay the bills. When he was finally arrested, Amanda and her brother were dumped back in the system. And apparently split up. Wife died within a year of Hugo going to prison."

"Kidney transplants are expensive," JJ said. "Did you interview Alvira ten years ago?"

"No. For some unknown reason, this information wasn't made available to the police." Mac slapped the file on the table. "But I've got Mr. Alvira coming in for an interview in about...." He glanced at his watch. "20 minutes."

"That's quick." JJ coughed, then walked over to her desk and grabbed a tissue. "I thought you said he was in jail?"

"He did a nickel then got an early release. Are you getting sick?"

"I think it might be a head cold starting. If you don't mind I'm going to take my lunch early and pick up something from the drug store. Stop this crud before it takes hold."

"Sure, go ahead." He pulled a ten dollar bill out of his jacket. "Can you pick me up some Tylenol for my back while you're out?"

JJ smiled. "No problem. I won't be long."

The bells on the office door jangled as she hurried out.

***

Mac shook hands with Hugo Alvira. First thing he noticed about the man was the ring finger on his right hand. Everything above the first joint was missing.

Mr. Alvira was in his early sixties, tall, balding, with a frail appearance. He looked like he would benefit from a few good meals. Mac had a passing thought that perhaps he should offer to move their meeting to the diner down the street.

Instead, he gestured toward the chair in front of his desk. "Mr. Alvira, thanks for meeting me. Can I get you a cup of coffee? I think we've got some fruit cake around here too."

"No thanks. Never developed a taste for either. You can call me Hugo." The man smiled and added, "My parole officer encouraged me to make the effort to meet with you...so to speak. What can I do for you?"

"Okay. Right to business. Tell me about Amanda Norman."

The man's smile disappeared. "Did you find her? Is she alive? I saw the newspaper stories–even in prison we got the news."

"No. I'm still looking for her." Mac watched the man.

"Poor little girl." Hugo's left leg began a nervous movement, his bony knee bouncing up and down.

"When was the last time you saw her?"

"Must be more than a dozen years ago. I was holding some items for a friend. How was I to know he stole them? Cops blamed me. Took my kids. Took all of them."

"Amanda and her brother weren't yours," Mac said. He'd heard that same story or a version of it from every thief he'd ever arrested.

"I know that. Felt like mine though." Hugo stared at Mac. "They were good kids. I tried to teach them things–things they needed to survive. I did right by them. We were happy. Then they were gone. And then my wife was gone. Broke her heart losing those kids. Me? I lost everything, but my memories."

He didn't believe a word of it. Mac could almost hear the violins playing in the background. The man's criminal record showed a history of property crimes and alcoholism. It was amazing he ever passed a background check to get the foster kids in the first place. "Did you hear from Amanda after you went to prison? How about after you got out?"

"No. Not a word." Hugo shook his head. "But if you find her, tell her to give her old Uncle Hugo a call. Be nice to see her one more time. My liver is failing. I probably won't be around for another Christmas. "

Mac still couldn't work up any sympathy for the man. "Tell me about Amanda? What was she like?"

An hour later Mac had learned very little, other than that Amanda was smart, resourceful, and devoted to her younger brother. He did solve the mystery of how Hugo got the kids in the first place. He hadn't. They had been placed with Lisa Alvira during one of the times that the couple had been separated. Social Services never bothered to check up on the family after he moved back in.

Mac also learned that what Hugo believed were "life skills" involved lock picking and by-passing alarm systems. Didn't take much reading between the lines to see that Hugo saw his "kids" as apprentice thieves. After an hour, Mac decided the man didn't know what had happened to Amanda after she left his care.

Mac watched him leave. He knew Hugo was lying to him, but he just didn't know about what.

***

"So you want to shake things up a bit, huh? Good for you. About time."

Rachel scanned the color wheel Katja, her twenty-something beautician with pink hair, had thrust in her hands. She was still trying to shake off Ella's criticisms of her life. But was she really ready to go blond? How about red? Her grandmother had redheads on her side of the family so maybe...

Rachel shook her head. Who was she kidding? She'd look like Raggedy Ann if she went red and Grams would have called her a Hotsy-Totsy if she went blond. Rachel grinned at the memory of her grandmother's opinion of those who bleached their hair. Tina, her ex-husband's then mistress, now fiancée, was definitely a Hotsy-Totsy or a skank, according to son Sam.

She handed the color wheel back to Katja.

"I think I just want to freshen things up. Maybe trim the ends and...get rid of the gray?"

Katja sighed.

Rachel knew she had disappointed the hairdresser with her conservative approach, but after all, it was her hair and she could only take so much change at a time.

Katja chewed her lip, then ran her fingers through Rachel's curls. "How about I give you some soft highlights and low lights. They'll give your hair some depth. I'll cut your hair—"

Rachel held up a hand. "But keep it long enough that I can pull it back in a ponytail when things get crazy."

Katja smiled. "Trust me. I get it. You're like my mother. You want to look like you, but better. I'll get some color swatches for you to pick from."

Rachel nodded. She had a date that night and for her first New Year's Eve date in, she had to think about that, how long had it been? For her first New Year's Eve date in 20 years. She wanted to look chic, maybe in the right lighting, even elegant. Okay she'd just settle for being the best she could considering her age and limited resources. She was rethinking her outfit choice. As a Christmas present Jeff and his wife Kathleen had given her a gift card to a fancy dress shop. She couldn't imagine a better time to use it.

By the time New Year's Eve rolled around, she'd like to think that Mac Sullivan wouldn't know what hit him.

She sat back in the chair. As for Aunt Ella, she'd show her too. The new Rachel Brenner was smart, independent, and attractive. She reached for the latest issue of *People* magazine, and well-informed too.

***

Although his life in general might tend to drift downhill, the road Mac was on didn't. He wasn't sure Jeff's Ford sedan was going to make it to the group home located in Arlington, Virginia, much less get him back to DC. The transmission whined again as he drove the last mile to the address Social Services had reluctantly given to Lt. Greeley when Mac had stopped by the station to ask another favor. He'd dropped off a few items he'd taken from Amanda Norman's box of belongings. Lt. Greeley had authorized a CSI technician to check for prints. With any luck, he'd have a good set to run through the criminal and government data bases.

Afternoons in late December got dark early. He was glad he found the group home while there was still light. It looked like most of the others on a block of tract homes built in the 1950s. The house numbers were hidden by a large Christmas wreath on the front door. There was a well-used basketball hoop attached to the garage. Three garbage cans sat at the curb waiting for trash collection the next day. Next to them was a green plastic container marked recyclables. Mac could see empty cans of soda in the bin as he walked up the sidewalk to the neatly kept two-story colonial, in the middle of a quiet suburb. There was no sign on the door to mark this house as a group home for developmentally disabled adults.

He'd barely knocked when the door opened.

"Who are you?" A young man dressed in jeans and sweatshirt looked at Mac expectantly.

"I'm looking for..." Mac checked his notes for the name of the Group Home Manager, "Melinda Jackson. She's expecting me."

"Mel, there's somebody here for you." The young man walked away from the door towards the back of the house.

Mac waited a moment, and then entered. A large Christmas tree with opened boxes under it sat in the corner of what he assumed was the communal living room. Not quite sure what to do, he waited a moment, debating calling Ms. Jackson on his cell phone when a tall, African-American woman rushed into the hallway.

"Mr. Sullivan? Sorry to keep you waiting. Charlene Carpenter of the Community Assessment Team called and said you'd be stopping by. Come on back to the kitchen."

He followed her down a hallway into an old, but clean kitchen. A long oak table with eight chairs dominated the center of the room. Two young men in their 20s were setting the table; a third was carefully stirring a pot of, judging from the smell, spaghetti sauce.

"Good job guys. Mark, turn down the flame under the sauce and just let it simmer."

She turned to the two men who had just finished putting out the dinner plates. "Is the salad ready? How about the garlic bread?"

"Check," said one of the young men, flinging open the refrigerator to reveal a large plastic bowl filled with lettuce and vegetables.

"The garlic bread's in the oven," said the other, looking closely at the timer. "It's got 5 more minutes before it's done."

"Okay, then. I think we're set. I'll call you when the timer goes off."

The young men left the kitchen.

Melinda Jackson pulled out two chairs from the table and motioned for Mac to sit.

The housemother took a sip of what looked like old, cold coffee. "I understand you're looking for Randell Norman."

"Yes, ma'am. I'm a private investigator. The files from Social Services were a little sketchy. I understand he's been living here for four years."

Melinda Jackson nodded. "That's right. Moved in here when the home opened. One of our first residents. Came here when he aged out of the foster care system."

"Could I talk to him? I've got some questions about his sister. "

"His sister?" The woman looked confused. "I'm not sure...I'm not sure that Randy will be much help. Do you know what Fetal Alcohol Syndrome is, Mr. Sullivan?"

Mac frowned. "Not much. Babies born from a mother who abused alcohol while pregnant? Affects their intelligence?"

Melinda Jackson took another sip of her coffee. "More than that. It's a lifelong condition. For Randy, he has trouble with daily activities like working, managing money, finding and keeping a job. He needs a consistent routine and a supportive community. He can barely remember what happened an hour ago. That's part of the syndrome. He has trouble expressing himself and gets very emotional if pressed. I think if you really need information about his sister, you should look elsewhere."

Just then the timer went off. Ms. Jackson rose and turned off the oven. "I've got to get the men in here for dinner. They handle the whole thing, from grocery shopping to cooking to cleaning up, but need supervision. We eat together as a family. Randy is part of our family. Do you want to join us?"

"No thank you. Do you think I could have a few moments with Randell, er Randy?"

Ms. Jackson checked her watch. "Come with me. Randy's in his room. We've got about 10 minutes until dinner. Routine is important. I don't want him to miss eating with the group and I don't want you upsetting him."

"No ma'am." Mac followed the manager up the stairs to the last room at the end of the hallway. Easy to see that Melinda Jackson ran a tight, very structured ship.

Ms. Jackson knocked on the door and waited for permission to enter. Mac could hear the bangs and whistles of a video game.

"Who's there?"

Ms. Jackson opened the door. A thin young man in his early 20s, with blond hair, lay on the bed, playing with a hand-held video game. "Randy, this is Mr. Sullivan. He wants to ask you a few questions about your sister."

The young man looked confused. "She's not here. Do you know her? Mel, have you seen her? Did you tell him she doesn't live here?"

Mac wasn't sure how to proceed. "When did you last see your sister?"

Randy looked at his watch in consternation. "I don't know. A long time ago. Is she lost? I didn't mean to lose her again."

The house manager sat down next to Randy on the bed and pulled him into a hug. "Shhhh, it's okay Randy. Why don't you go wash your hands and go down to dinner? It's spaghetti night. Is it your turn to dry the dishes?"

The young man calmed down. "I do a good job drying the dishes. Best in the house. You said that."

"That's right. Now don't forget about washing your hands."

Randy got up and left the room.

Mac followed Melinda Jackson back down the stairs to the front door.

Ms. Jackson opened the front door. "He has very little sense of time. Sometimes he remembers what day it is, sometimes he doesn't. I understand that the family was split up when Randy was just eight or nine. Mother died of an overdose; fathers, I think each kid had a different Dad, nowhere to be found."

Mac felt defeated. "I appreciate your help. I'll keep looking, but it's almost impossible to find anyone who knew Amanda well. Randy isn't the only one with memory problems."

He started down the walk to his car.

"Mr. Sullivan?"

Mac turned and saw the housemother standing on the front porch.

"Let me have your business card. I'll leave it for Mandy when she comes next Sunday."

Mac froze. "What?"

She stepped off the porch and walked towards him. "If you want to talk to Randy's sister directly, I'll have Andrea Hudson, the regular weekend housemother, give her your card next weekend. Mandy can call you."

Mac jogged back, almost sliding into her on the icy drive. "Give her my...How? His sister has been missing a long time. You know where she is?"

"No. There must be a mistake." Melinda Jackson looked confused. "Missing? What happened? I've never met her but I've talked to her dozens of times on the telephone. She comes on the weekends and I'm usually off then. But with the holidays, I've been....Andrea says that Mandy comes every other Sunday to take Randy out. Mandy's missing? Oh, my! I thought this was just some kind of background check for a job. I understand you're a private investigator? Are the police looking for–"

"Mandy?" Mac felt like he'd fallen down the rabbit hole. "Is her real name Amanda?

"Maybe." Melinda shrugged. "Randy always calls her Mandy. Why?"

"And this Andrea person has seen her?" Mac found his voice. "Can you tell me how I can talk to her, the other housemother? I want to–did you say you have Amanda's contact information?"

"Mel, you coming. It's time. Time for dinner."

Mel turned to the voices calling her from the kitchen. "I'll be right there. Hold your horses."

Mac heard laughter as the young men made whinnying sounds.

She frowned at Mac. "Come with me. Andrea is on vacation, visiting family in Germany. She won't be back until next weekend. Maybe you should just call Amanda yourself."

They went back into the house and Melinda Jackson walked over to a desk, pulled out a folder, and hastily wrote down the information. "I just have a phone number for Mandy. I hope she's alright."

Mac stared at the information he'd spent 10 years searching for.

Chapter 6

The drive back to DC was cold and slow. Snow was falling in earnest and the traffic was almost at a standstill.

He pulled out his cell phone and called the office.

"Sullivan Investigations, if it's not illegal and you're paying cash, we'll do it."

"JJ, damn it! You don't really answer the phone that way!"

"Of course not. I always mention that we also take personal checks and Visa."

"JJ!" No wonder his business was just squeaking by. That little speech also explained the kinds of cases they kept getting.

"Chill out. We have caller I.D., Mac. I knew it was you."

"Sorry." He sighed "I seemed to have misplaced my sense of humor. I need you to check out a phone number for me." He rattled off the number that Melinda Jackson had given him. "Don't call it yet; just see if you can find out the address and how long the phone has been in service."

There was silence on the other end of the line.

Damn cell company. Another dropped call. Or maybe he'd forgotten to pay his cell phone bill. No, he could hear something moving.

"JJ? Are you there?"

"Yeah. Sorry. Got it. Just had to find a pen that works. I'm at your desk and you have a cup full of pens without ink. Why do you save–"

The weather was getting worse and he didn't have time for the "dried-up pen" discussion again. "I'm going to be at least another hour, maybe two, depending on the weather. Can you take Whiskey home with you and I'll pick her up there on my way to Rachel's?"

"Can't do it," JJ said. "Sorry, I've got the bike today, remember? And I'll never get a cab with her in tow. Some people have large canine prejudices. We'll just stay here until you get here. I'll order a pizza...or two delivered."

"Okay, thanks." Mac started to hang up, then changed his mind, "Wait, JJ?"

"Yeah, boss?"

"No anchovies for Whiskey. I mean it. They give her gas."

The headlights from a...truck–or one of those damn SUV he was now seeing everywhere, thanks to Edgar–appeared in his rearview mirror, blinding him.

Mac ended the call, adjusted the mirror, and attempted to turn down the heater. The Ford's heater was the one thing that seemed to work well, too well. Unfortunately the interior lights didn't work at all and he couldn't find the fan control.

He was leaning over, looking at the dash when the SUV's engine revved and the vehicle rear-ended him.

The next thing he knew the Ford was pushed into the old pickup truck ahead of him and the airbag exploded against his face and chest.

***

Jeff O'Herlihy shut the lid on his laptop and looked over at his wife who was preparing a casserole at their kitchen island. He couldn't help thinking she was a pretty as the day he met her. All long legs, red hair, and a smile that would light up a room. He was a lucky man and he knew it.

"Kathleen, my love, we're going to rebuild bigger and better than ever."

The fire at the O'Herlihy Funeral Home had destroyed all but the important things: his family, his employees, and his friends. His insurance agent fell into one or more of those categories, depending on the day and the particular claim.

"Why?" Kathleen O'Herlihy, mother of four, turned to face her husband.

"Why do you want to rebuild? O'Herlihy's was a family business. Your father inherited it from his father. You inherited it from yours. None of our kids are interested in mortuary science. What's the point? The insurance money means you could retire if you wanted."

"The point?" He couldn't believe she was asking him that. "The point is I'm too young to retire. We still have to get Sean through college. And what seems like a lot of money now, might not last since I plan for us to live forever."

"Jeff! I'm serious."

"Kathleen, if I'd wanted to give it up, I would have sold out to Dalton Funeral Homes. Why do you think I fought so hard to keep the business? It wasn't just a pissing match between me and Fletcher Dalton."

"I don't know what this business really means to you. After all these years you finally have a chance to be free, to do what you want, not what your father expected you to do. Tell me why you want to rebuild. Why you want to be permanently on call. I can't remember the last time we went on vacation for more than three days. While you're spending long hours at the Funeral Home, I'm left here alone, trying to figure out how to fill my time. It wasn't so bad when all the kids were home, but now...Explain why we have to keep on this treadmill."

So that was it. The gaping chasm between them. He got up from the kitchen table and moved to stand in front of her, the granite top of the kitchen island and thirty years of love between them.

"Kathleen, I've always been doing what I wanted. This business is more than some burden my father passed on to me. I like what I do. I help the living get through the worst moments of their life and I make sure the deceased go out of this world with dignity and respect. And you know what? All jokes aside, I'm good at what I do."

"Yes, you are. I appreciate that you take pride in your work, but wouldn't you like a change? I know I would. When Sean graduates from high school, wouldn't it be nice to be able to travel? See something besides DC?"

Jeff's cell phone rang and from the ring tone both of them knew who was calling.

Jeff shrugged. "Probably needs another car."

Kathleen grimaced. "When has he not?"

"Well, that's one thing that is going to change. He's making noises about buying one of his own."

"Yeah, right. Go ahead and talk to him," Kathleen said, putting foil wrap over the casserole pan and putting it in the freezer for another day. "You've already made up your mind anyway about the funeral home."

"He can leave a message." Jeff sighed. "Tell you what, let's continue this discussion tomorrow. Maybe I could hire more help with the embalming, free up more of my time. We could plan a trip for next year, maybe go to Dublin and see your cousins like you wanted."

Kathleen shrugged. "I'll believe that when I see it."

"Let's go to bed," Jeff suggested, moving to take her in his arms. "For a smile, I'll let you have your way with me."

Kathleen hugged him back. "We're not done talking about this, Jeff."

Jeff held on tight. "I know. We'll figure it out. That's what we do. We figure it out together."

***

"Sorry to get you out this time of night. I tried calling Jeff but he wasn't picking up."

Mac, seated in the hospital emergency waiting room, slowly got to his feet as Rachel approached.

He could see her already pale skin go stark white.

"What happened? Are you okay? You look...look." She gestured towards him.

Mac glanced down at the bloodstains splattered on his clothes. He knew every bone in his body ached, but he didn't think it was so bad that Rachel would be left speechless. He scanned the room for a mirror, then thought better of it. He eased back down in the chair.

"I was the filling in a hot metal sandwich."

Rachel sat down next to him and ran her fingers through her curls, stopping abruptly. Mac recognized that Rachel Brenner gesture of exasperation.

"Guy rear-ended me and pushed me into a pickup truck which was stopped. Airbag exploded and...."

Rachel nodded and reached for her hair, but stopped again. "Have you been seen? How long have you been waiting? What do the doctors say?"

Mac also recognized Rachel Brenner in full-on worry mode, immediately followed by indignation mode. He held up his hand, hoping to avoid anger mode. He didn't need her picking a fight with the hospital staff.

"I'm fine. Sore as hell, but according to the docs, nothing broken, just bruised. I'm going to have a couple of black eyes and a swollen nose. I was going to get a cab, but–"

Rachel rose. "No, no. I'm glad you called. I was beginning to think I was being stood up again. So what if our date is at a hospital, it wouldn't be the first time." She grinned, softening the effect of her words.

Mac shook his head and thought for at least the thousandth time, he really needed to figure out this boyfriend stuff. "Sorry. I didn't intend to screw up yet another date."

"Never mind. I've adjusted my expectations." She flashed him another grin.

He chuckled. "I may surprise you sometime."

"No doubt about it." Rachel held out a hand to help Mac stand. "Are you hungry? I've got some beef and barley soup in the freezer at home. I can heat it up. I think there's even some garlic bread."

"What do you get out of this relationship? You cook and I hobble around, trying to recover from some injury."

Rachel took Mac by the elbow and started walking. "You're right. In the few months I've known you, Mr. Sullivan, that seems to have happened with some regularity. Car wrecks, shootings, plumbing mistakes–"

Mac snorted. "Thanks for the memories."

***

The snow was really coming down. It was going to be midnight by the time they got back to DC. He'd called JJ again after the accident. She'd assured him that she and Whiskey were fine and were spending the evening watching the Smithsonian gift shop's digital surveillance files. She also mentioned that the phone number he'd given her earlier was to a disposable cell phone. No way to trace it.

"Earth to Mac?"

"Huh?" He'd been thinking about the case and missed Rachel's question.

"I asked you about Jeff's car. Where is it?"

Mac grimaced. "Towed and ready for salvage. The man is going to—"

Rachel laughed. "Lend you another one when you need it."

Mac eased into the seat of Rachel's Jeep and leaned back against the headrest. "I'm not so sure about that. My track record with his fleet is dismal. I'm going to have to buy a car this year. It's past time." He glanced around her vehicle. "Maybe I'll get something like this. Everyone seems to be driving one."

"Get the heated seat option. Whiskey would love that." Rachel slid into the driver's seat, switched on the interior lights and checked the car mirror. She took a moment to rearrange her curls, while running the defroster.

Something was different, but Mac was at a loss. "Did you change something? New coat? Perfume? Teeth? You…you had your teeth whitened. They definitely look brighter."

Rachel gave him a withering glance and started the engine. "Did the accident affect your brain, Mr. Sullivan? Teeth whitening as a compliment?"

Mac knew he had entered a minefield, but just wasn't quite sure where to put down his foot without setting off an explosion.

He thought for a moment. "Haircut. That's it, isn't it? Looks nice."

He saw Rachel relax and thought maybe he'd carefully tap-danced his way to safety.

Rachel eased into traffic. "Well, I did have a little cut off. Katja, she's my hairdresser, called it shaping, but there sure seemed to be a lot of my hair on the floor."

"Glad you kept it a color I recognize. Some women go crazy with the dyeing and bleaching and...." He saw Rachel's frown and figured that somehow he'd stepped back into danger. "But your hair, it looks like you."

He thought he caught a hint of a smile. "And that's nice."

The smile got bigger.

"Know much about hair dyes Mr. Sullivan. Tried any of that Grecian Formula yourself?"

Mac self-consciously ran his fingers through his graying, thinning hair. "Nope. It is what it is."

Rachel reached over and patted his hand. "And that's very nice too."

Maybe it was the painkillers, but Mac was starting to feel better.

They stopped at a red light. The snow was still coming down. The wipers on the Jeep were sliding back and forth. Watching them move the large white flakes was almost hypnotic. It had been a long day, he was tired, but his mind was still trying to process everything that he'd learned. Was Amanda Norman alive? Had someone deliberately tried to kill him? Lost in thought, he suddenly realized he'd missed the last few words Rachel had said. Something else about her hair?

"Sorry, what?"

Rachel laughed. "I was just telling you about my hairdresser. She's actually a blonde. But she has pink hair. At least today she did. A couple of months ago it was lavender. Come to think of it, I think she colors it to match her outfit. She was wearing a pink sweater today, so—"

Mac reached out for Rachel's hand. "Wait! Stop."

The light turned green.

Rachel looked worried. "You need me to pull over. Are you going to be sick?"

"No. I just need you to say that again."

Worry turned to confusion. "Say what?"

A car behind them honked and Rachel accelerated.

Mac said slowly, "Tell me about your hairdresser."

"Well she's about 24. Her name is Katja, which I think is Swedish or maybe Norwegian, but of course, she's actually from Silver Spring."

Mac shook his head. "No, tell me about her hair."

"Her hair?" Rachel giggled. "Her hair is pink and sometimes lavender, and occasionally, around Halloween, she dyes it black. Why?"

"So she might not be blond at all?"

"Katja? Well, I guess it could be a different color. But given her coloring, I think she's probably light-haired. Why does it matter?

Mac tried to keep things straight in his mind, but the painkillers really were making him sleepy. Blond haired girls could be any color they wanted. So could Amanda Norman. Maybe Amanda did more than cut her hair? He needed to talk with Andrea Hudson, have her describe Randy's sister. Maybe he could get her to come into the police station when she got back and sit with a sketch artist or whatever the computer equivalent to a sketch artist was called these days.

Tomorrow he would call Lt. Greeley. Find out if he knew someone who could do an age progression photo of Amanda—one with different hair lengths and hair colors. Then perhaps he'd know if Amanda Norman was really still alive or, the more likely scenario, if someone was impersonating a long dead teenager.

Chapter 7

The first thought he had was a firm realization that he was old. Old and infirm. Old and a wuss. Okay, that was more than one thought, but it all circled back to the fact that he couldn't handle the action component of being a private investigator. There wasn't a bone, muscle, tendon, or hangnail in his body that didn't ache.

His second thought was that something smelled really good and it definitely wasn't a Jimmy Dean Sausage Patty.

And his final thought, before opening his eyes, was that once again Mac Sullivan was sleeping in one of Rachel Brenner's beds, but it wasn't her bedroom. He opened bleary eyes and judging from the Black Sabbath poster and the University of Pennsylvania mug on the desk, he assumed he was in Sam Brenner's bedroom. He did remember Rachel telling him that her son was away for the week. Something about a ski resort.

This led him back to his original thought. He was old, old, old, because he was still in the guest bedroom like he was 16 and staying over after a well-chaperoned prom.

It took him a depressing three minutes before he could get himself upright and out of bed. He looked down and realized he was wearing Penn sweat pants and a Black Sabbath T-shirt.

His mortification was complete when he recognized the freshly-laundered clothes on the desk chair were the ones he'd worn the day before. He prayed that he had been conscious enough to have changed himself. If he didn't hurt so badly, he'd swear off the pain meds.

He gingerly made his way downstairs and into the kitchen. He paused at the kitchen door and watched for a moment. Rachel was moving from refrigerator to counter to oven, measuring, stirring, tasting, and finally nodding, a pleased look on her face. Whiskey was lounging next to kitchen table; she'd picked a spot where she could monitor all the food preparation and watch the cat sitting on top of the refrigerator. JJ must have dropped off the dog, maybe this morning? Or maybe Rachel picked her up? He didn't know and surprisingly didn't care. Just happy Whiskey was here and so was he. The scene of domesticity made Mac feel…he couldn't quite put his finger on what he was feeling. Oh yeah, old…and hungry.

He shuffled into the warm kitchen and was rewarded with a bright smile from Rachel, a woof from his dog, and a hiss from Snickers.

"You're finally awake. It's after noon. You were dead to the world when I checked on you earlier. If you'll excuse the undertaker humor. Jeff's bad jokes have taken root. I can't help myself."

Mac scraped a hand over his grizzled face. "Sorry to impose. I seem to do that a lot."

Rachel slid a steaming cup of coffee across the table. "Don't be ridiculous. Drink this. It's bound to help. What's your pleasure? Eggs? Bacon? Hash browns? Coffeecake's got another ten minutes before it comes out of the oven."

He decided he was too old and feeble to do anything but surrender. Besides he was unexpectedly hungry. To Whiskey's dismay, he ate everything Rachel put in front of him.

When at last he pushed back the plate, dusted with just a few crumbs of an amazing blueberry coffee cake, he didn't feel quite so old.

Rachel held out the pill bottle. "Painkillers as an after-breakfast chaser?"

Mac shook his head. "Got any Advil? Those pills make me loopy."

"Yeah, that much was obvious."

Mac couldn't figure out what Rachel's smile meant and decided he didn't want to know.

At last, she sat down at the table, the pot of coffee between them. "So Mr. Sullivan, what's on the agenda for today?"

"I've got to face the music and talk to Jeff."

Rachel laughed. "Done. I called him this morning, he yelled for a good five minutes, and then said he'd leave the keys to an old ice cream truck at the office."

"Thanks. You definitely took one for the team."

He hoped she didn't mind that he'd added her to his team.

"Do you know what I did with the police report of the accident?"

Rachel reached across to the counter and grabbed a handful of papers. Mac scanned them quickly.

"Looks like the guy in the SUV took off before the cops arrived."

Rachel took a sip of coffee. "Maybe he wasn't insured."

Mac shook his head. "I can't decide if I'm getting paranoid or my old Spidey senses are still in gear, but I think somebody wanted to send me a message."

"I'll bite. What's the message?"

Mac shrugged. "I wish I knew exactly. Obviously they want to scare me off doing something. Or I guess it could be someone I arrested from when I was a cop. Someone really angry. People hold long grudges."

"Okay," Rachel said slowly. "Let's stick with the first option. Scare you to stop doing what? Investigating a case? What case?"

"I'm not sure. I've got a couple of active cases on-going, some divorce stuff that JJ insists we take for the money, but mostly I've been spending my time trying to solve a missing teen case that's ten years old."

Mac quickly filled her in on the details of the Amanda Norman case.

"So do you think it's Amanda who's trying to scare you? And why send you postcards to find her if now that you're trying to do just that, she tries to kill you? And if it's not Amanda, who else wants to find her? Or who doesn't want you to find her? And what if she's dead? Could this be her killer going after you?"

Mac held up his hands to ward off Rachel's verbal assault.

"I don't know the answers to any of your excellent questions. The one thing I do know is that if this hit-and-run is associated with the Amanda Norman case, I should find out what happened to her before anybody else gets hurt."

Rachel took a sip of her coffee. "Is it possible that Amanda Norman is dead and that the postcards are from somebody who wants you to find the killer?"

"No, well...maybe. The brother definitely sees someone who claims to be his sister every few weeks, but of course it could be someone impersonating Amanda. I don't know how reliable the brother is. He was young when they were separated, but I'd think he'd know his own sister, even if they'd been separated for four or five years."

Rachel shrugged. "People believe what they want to believe. He might just want to believe the woman who visits him is his sister. The better question is why would someone impersonate Amanda?"

Mac thought a moment. "Because they think the brother knows something or has something of value and they need access to him."

Mac finished his coffee and pushed back from the table.

"Actually all I've got are questions and so far, no answers. I'm going to get cleaned up and head over to my office. I'll call a cab."

Rachel stood up. "Don't be silly. I'll drive you. Jeff doesn't need me at work today and you don't want to drive an old ice cream truck do you? It's out of season."

He managed a chuckle. "Thanks again…for everything. And if you truly don't have anything better to do, I'd love a chauffeur. Give me twenty minutes. "

Mac headed up the stairs, when he heard, "I washed all your clothes. Got the blood out of everything. You should probably think about hitting the after-Christmas sales for some new underwear. Yours is kind of ratty."

Mac considered whether anyone had ever died of total, abject humiliation. Probably not, but at that moment, it seemed a preferable alternative to continuing to live.

***

The offices of Sullivan Investigations were empty. And probably the entire building too.

Rachel followed Mac and Whiskey inside. The old building had one other tenant, a dentist who had moved in the month before. She'd met him once on the stairs. According to Edgar, Dr. Felix Payne had leased a small three-room office unit on the floor right above theirs. She couldn't imagine why a dentist would want to be in this part of town. Of course the answer might be the same as to why Mac had an office there, real estate prices in DC were still sky high. As Edgar had suggested, if her aunt wanted to invest in something, she should buy property.

"Or she could just keep the farm," Rachel mumbled, hanging her coat on the clothes tree near the entrance.

"What?" Mac handed her his jacket.

"Nothing. Just thinking aloud. Can I turn up the thermostat?"

"You can try. The landlord promised to get a new furnace but so far nothing. JJ talked to him again last week. He managed to put her off, no easy feat. I guess I'll have to deal with him soon. He put in the elevator for Edgar, so I didn't want to push too hard. And he likes Whiskey. Was hoping that with the dentist here now, he would invest some money in additional remodeling."

"Everyone likes Whiskey." She glanced into Mac's office at the wolfhound who had crawled up on the green futon. Leaning against the doorframe, she added, "And Mac, he didn't put in the elevator for Edgar. He did it to stay in compliance with accessibility codes. Heat is also something he's responsible for providing. Don't let this slide."

Mac shrugged. "I just know what it's like to have a cash flow problem."

Shivering, Rachel crossed the room and grabbed a sweater that JJ had left hanging on her desk chair. "I bet Jeff knows someone who could get him a deal. Want me to get involved?"

"No." His grin softened his answer. "I'll deal with it."

Right, she thought. He'll deal with it like he does with buying cars and replacing underwear. Put it off as long as possible. She made a mental note to wait a few days, and then ask JJ for the landlord's contact information.

"What can I do to help you?" She walked over to the white board and scanned the timeline for Amanda Norman's disappearance.

"If you could figure out JJ's new coffeemaker and get that started, I'll see if I can set up the laptop to play the footage from the Smithsonian gift shop. JJ said she watched it, but I need to watch it too. I might recognize someone from the earlier investigation. You could keep me company? Another set of eyes might help."

"Sure." She figured she could give it an hour or two, if it got too boring; she had a book in her purse.

***

Five hours later, Mac was seriously thinking of joining Whiskey on the futon for a nap. His neck was stiff from the after-effects of the wreck, his large breakfast was long gone, and he had to admit that Rachel was right; the office was too chilly for comfort.

Watching the black and white security footage was almost as much fun as watching paint dry. So far he'd seen a few people who looked familiar, but upon reflection he realized that was only because some were repeat customers at the gift shop; in other words he didn't recognize them from anywhere other than the gift shop. The security camera took an image every 30 seconds, so looking at the footage wasn't like viewing a movie; it was more like viewing a series of digital photos. There were four angles for each timeframe.

"This is probably a waste of time," Mac announced. "I'm sorry, you must be bored out of your mind."

"There are certainly a large number of postcard sales. Many from the rack with those limited edition cards." Rachel stood up and stretched. "I guess postcards are popular because they're cheap souvenirs. The only person I saw that looked even slightly suspicious was the tall, skinny guy wearing one of those team jackets and a baseball cap. The sleeves were too short for his long arms."

Mac knew who she was talking about. The man wearing the NY Jets sports jacket and cap. He had been alone and had gone straight towards the postcard rack after entering the shop. Mac had chalked it up to the man being in a rush to grab a souvenir and get out. "What was suspicious about him? Besides his ill-fitting clothes?"

"I'm not sure. Something just seemed off. Something about his hands."

***

"That's him," Mac said. It took him almost an hour to find the correct frames. He made a mental note for any future viewing of digital tapes–always jot down the date and time of any frame you might want to watch again. He stared at the four viewing angles, all showing a man in an oversized Jets team jacket with too short sleeves buying a postcard. The man also wore a ball cap that shaded his face from view. One identifying feature couldn't be hidden by any disguise; the man was very tall.

He admitted to himself that the only reason he had paid any special attention to the man was the fact that the cap hid the man's face. Out of all the people who had purchased cards, his was the only face missing from the monitor screen.

Mac continued to watch for some way to gauge the suspect's height. He'd need to make another trip to the gift shop, measure the height of the postcard rack from the floor to be sure, but he was guessing several inches more than six-foot.

"Sorry, I can't make out his face," Rachel said. "How will this help you?"

"Can you freeze it there?" Mac got up and moved closer to the computer screen. "I see what you mean about his hand. Look as he pays for the cards."

Because the security footage was in black and white, he hadn't noticed the first time. The man was missing a finger.

Mac walked over to the white board and drew a circle around one name. "I think I might know who has been sending me postcards."

***

It was going to take almost 90 minutes for the Chinese place down the street to deliver their order. If he was lucky. Mac didn't consider himself a lucky person. So the ETA on the food was probably going to be closer to two hours. With the snowy weather, the owner had warned that his one delivery driver was running way behind. Mac suspected that if he hadn't been a regular customer, Mr. Ling would have refused outright another delivery order.

While they waited for their dinner, Mac and Rachel figured out how to print off screen snaps of the suspect. A hungry Whiskey supervised closely.

"Maybe JJ can do her magic and enhance these," Rachel suggested. "If Hugo Alvira is sending you postcards, then maybe he's working with that woman posing as Amanda at the group home. Have you interviewed Amanda Norman's classmates? Maybe the woman is someone who was friends with Amanda."

"She didn't have any friends."

"There must have been someone." Rachel walked over to the table with all the files stacked on it. "What's in the box?"

He'd forgotten to go through the rest of the box of Amanda Norman's personal effects. After pulling out a hairbrush and a hand mirror from the top of the box to take to Greeley for prints, he'd neglected to inventory the rest of the contents. He was getting old.

"Amanda Norman's belongings. Stuff that was left at the Miller house. Louise Miller gave it to me. I haven't been through it yet."

He joined Rachel at the table.

Mac opened the lid. "Not much in here. Some old clothes."

Rachel lifted out several pairs of well-worn blue jeans, a pair of white tennis shoes, a half dozen simple cotton tops, three sets of cheap underwear, a plastic bag with half-used toiletries, three dog-eared paperback romance books, and a shoebox filled with the kinds of junk you'd find in a desk drawer.

He sorted through the shoebox. "No photographs in here. A few ticket stubs from concerts. Maybe five dollars in coins. A couple of crumpled receipts from a drugstore. A note from a teacher asking for a parent to set up an appointment. What do you think? Seems like Amanda didn't have much stuff for a teenage girl. Even one in foster care."

Rachel picked up the receipts. She looked from the receipts to the white board. "The dates on these are just before she went missing according to your timeline."

If he hadn't been so tired, he would have picked up on that. "What did she buy?"

"Some cosmetics, nail scissors, and hair color," Rachel answered. "None of those items are in this box. I'd bet she had more clothes than this too. I think Amanda planned to run away. I think she packed a bag with the stuff that was important to her and just left."

Whiskey paced back and forth, whining.

Mac watched as the dog stopped and stared at the door.

"Did you hear something girl? I bet you're hungry too. Maybe Mr. Ling's delivery guy remembered that I'm a big tipper and put us at the front of the line."

Rachel laughed. "Big tipper? Maybe if this was still the 1970s."

Even Whiskey gave him a skeptical look.

"Hey, I'm not cheap," he argued. "I just have limited resources."

The ding sound of the elevator doors opening confirmed that someone else was in the building.

Mac pulled out his wallet. "Uh....Rachel do you have any cash? Small bills? I've just got twenties. Mr. Ling doesn't let his drivers carry cash so he won't be able to make change."

"I'll get this," Rachel offered, grabbing her purse and crossing the room to the door. She opened it and called back over her shoulder, "You can save your money for our fancy New Year's Eve date. I'm expecting something special."

Later Mac would tell Lieutenant Greeley that it seemed the next three things happened at the same time, although he suspected that there really was a logical progression from the first to the last. He knew this was true because if they really had happened at the same time, he'd probably be dead.

Rachel had barely gotten the word "special" out when all hell broke loose.

Whiskey bumped into his arm as she launched herself at Rachel, knocking her to the floor.

He dropped his wallet and leaned down behind JJ's desk to pick it up.

Someone in a ski mask stood in the doorway and fired a gun at him.

Chapter 8

"The good news is that we're not sitting in another emergency room tonight," Rachel said, her fingers buried in Whiskey's fur.

"It's not night," Mac reminded her. "3:30 am. is technically morning, we missed lunch and dinner, and a police station isn't much better than an ER. I'm not seeing much good news here."

"You're alive to complain about all that and I'm here to listen. Really a miracle if you think about it." Rachel sighed.

"I might be running out of miracles. That's twice someone has tried to kill me this week and twice they've gotten away. You know what they say about the 'third time'."

They were sitting in Greeley's office waiting for him to come back with a ballistics report on the slug a crime scene tech had pulled out of JJ's old desk. Ironically, JJ's penchant for buying 1940s furniture and rehabbing it had saved his life. The bullet would have gone through a modern press wood desk like a knife through butter.

"So, day before yesterday, whoever tried to kill you by means of a hit-and-run car accident has moved on to a more direct method? Got to give the guy points for determination. Wonder what the rush is. Maybe he's got a big New Year's Eve date and wants to check you off his 'to-do' list, literally."

Mac whipped around to look at Rachel so fast that he was pretty sure he'd reinjured his already aching neck. "Are you trying to make me feel better because if so, you might want to work on your Susie Sunshine imitation."

Rachel's grin only served to make him feel worse. He rubbed the back of his neck, but the muscles were so tight that he was pretty sure that even an Eagle Scout couldn't undo the knot. He needed another pain pill. Something from that prescription bottle in his jacket pocket. But he'd just have to wait.

"What do you know that someone doesn't want you to know?"

"I wish I knew." Mac winced at the wording. Sounded cheesy. "I'm either close to finding something that is supposed to remain hidden or...."

Rachel tapped Mac's arm. "Or what? You either have uncovered a big secret or what?"

"Or I don't know. Maybe someone really doesn't like me." Mac suddenly stood up and started pacing. "Tell me again exactly what happened when the shooter came in."

"I didn't see anything. Whiskey knocked me to the ground and a gun went off." She ran her hand through the big dog's fur and whispered. "Thank you sweetheart."

Mac shook his head. "No. You did see something. That's just the shock talking. Close your eyes. Picture the scene in slow motion."

"It's not shock, thank you very much. I didn't see anything. You probably saw more than I did."

"Stop talking and close your eyes. Think, Rachel, what do you see?"

"I don't like your tone." Rachel crossed her arms across her chest. "Don't yell at me. I'm not one of your perps. And I don't take orders, I don't work for you."

Mac took a deep breath. "Sorry. I'm not feeling great right now. I'm sorry. It's just that I think you really did see the guy holding the gun and don't realize it. Just try it my way. Please."

She didn't unclench her arms, but Rachel closed her eyes.

He could see the furrows on her forehead as she appeared to concentrate on the scary events of earlier in the night.

"I started to walk to the door to get the Chinese food."

"Good," Mac said, "then what?"

Rachel opened her eyes. "Then Whiskey knocked me to the floor and I heard the gun go off."

Mac blew out a breath. "Try again."

Rachel looked at him, her eyes narrowed.

He gave her a small smile. "Please try again. Tell me everything you saw and this time tell me what you heard."

Rachel closed her eyes. "Okay, I started toward the door and heard growling…I mean I heard Whiskey growl. I didn't see her, but I could…I had the sensation that she was moving."

Rachel opened her eyes again. "Does that make sense? I didn't actually see her move, but it was like the air in the room was disturbed."

Mac nodded his encouragement. "Good. Keep going."

Rachel closed her eyes again. "I...I looked at Whiskey who was sort of in mid-leap and then glanced at the door....Wait, the door is open and a man is standing there...a man with a gun."

Rachel's eyes flew open. "Wow. You were right."

"Every once in a while I am." Mac smiled. "Tell me about the man with the gun."

"I only saw him for a second...no, not even that long. What is it, a millisecond? And then Whiskey had me down on the floor and I heard the gun go off. Next thing I knew, Whiskey was chasing the guy down the hall, and you called her to come back."

"I didn't want her to get hurt. Crazy guy could have shot her."
Rachel nodded.

"Now try and describe the guy. You know now that you saw him. What did he look like?"

"He was just standing there, dressed in black, with a black ski mask on. I couldn't even tell you the color of his hair, because it was covered."

"How tall? Compare it to the height of the door which is six foot-eight inches."

"Maybe five-eight or nine. Not real tall, but not overly short either."

"You sure?"

She glared at him. "Sure? No, I'm-"

"Sorry. Forget I said that." He nodded. "Sorry. Let's keep going. "Weight?"

"He was wearing sweat pants and a sweatshirt, but he didn't look either too fat or too skinny."

"Race?"

"He was covered from head-to-toe so I've got no idea…wait a minute, yes, I do. His hand, the one holding the gun. It was pale. He's Caucasian."

Rachel smiled at Mac. "Maybe I saw more than I thought."

For the first time in hours, Mac relaxed.

"Describe the hand to me. Anything unusual about it?"

Rachel clenched her eyes shut. She was silent for a few minutes and then said, "Mac, you know what? The man had all his fingers."

Again, she opened her eyes and looked straight at him. "That's what you wanted to know, isn't it? The man at the gift shop was missing a finger on his right hand. But the shooter had all five fingers. It couldn't be that man...that Hugo Alvira. So who wants you dead?"

"Lots of people," said a voice from the doorway. "I've wanted to kill him myself on many occasions."

Lieutenant James Greeley entered his office. "Here's what I know. The bullet we dug out of your assistant's desk doesn't match anything in our records. But I checked that recent break-in case you mentioned. Turns out the bullet that killed Louise Miller comes from the same gun that was used in a murder ten years ago, stolen in a robbery a few months before that."

Mac felt himself getting impatient. He wanted Greeley to reveal what he knew. "So who was the thief who stole the gun and killed somebody ten years ago?"

Greeley held up his well-manicured hand. "Not so fast. We know who did the robbery, but the murder weapon was never found. So Hugo Alvira went away for a string of robberies, but we couldn't tie him to the murder. Looks like maybe he had an accomplice."

"I'm confused." Rachel pulled on Mac's arm. "Why is a stranger trying so hard to kill you?"

Mac looked at Greeley and then at Rachel. "I haven't got a clue. Come on, I'll take you home."

Rachel pulled on her coat. "You'll stay with me until we figure out what's going on."

Mac shook his head. "Don't be silly. I'm fine and I don't want you in the middle of this."

"Might be a good idea," Greeley interjected. "Shooter might think that Rachel saw something. I'll beef up the patrols in her neighborhood."

Mac thought a moment, and then nodded. He didn't like it. Didn't like any of it.

***

"What are you doing up? It's not even 7 a.m. yet. You couldn't have gotten more than a couple hours sleep."

Mac looked up from the scribbles he'd been making on a legal pad. Rachel was standing in the doorway to her kitchen. Only the light over the stove was on and he was struck, not for the first time, how beautiful she was, and even more amazing that she didn't know it.

He shook his head to clear it. Insomnia and near-death experiences were making him soft.

"Couldn't sleep. Why are you awake? You were stuck in that police station too."

Rachel smiled. "Snickers sounded the alarm. She told me someone was in her kitchen. She's quite the 'watch cat,' you know."

"Sorry." He sighed. "Hope you don't mind, I made some coffee."

Rachel smiled. "No problem. You hungry? I could–"

"I'm fine. Don't go to any trouble. I'm just going over everything again and again, getting nowhere fast."

Rachel poured herself a cup of coffee and sat down across from him. "Walk it through for me. I'm confused. Are there two different people after you? Two different cases? All related? Does this long-lost missing girl have something to do with it? What's the story with the postcards and the guy with the missing finger? Is it all a coincidence that it's happening now? And are we still going out to dinner for New Year's Eve 'cuz I broke down and splurged on a nice dress."

Mac chuckled. "Maybe you meant to put that last one first."

Rachel grinned. "Maybe I did. I've got an appointment for a manicure too."

"Well the short answer is I don't know. As for the rest of your questions...." He started to tick off the facts on his fingers. "Every

Christmas, for ten years, somebody has sent me a postcard asking, 'Where is Amanda Norman.' But this year, this somebody knew I had retired from the force, had opened my own company, and knew the office address."

Rachel looked confused. "Does that mean it's somebody you know?"

Mac shook his head. "There was a photo in the newspaper last year at my retirement ceremony. If you plugged in my name in an Internet search, you'd know I wasn't on the Force now. A couple more clicks and you'd have found my new company and address. So, long story short, I don't think it's necessarily someone I know, but again, I can't be sure."

Rachel nodded and he continued.

"Hugo Alvira knew Amanda Norman and bought the same postcard that was sent to me this year. The fact that the wording on the postcard was the same as the others, leads me to believe he sent all the postcards...or had someone send them."

"So Hugo, the guy with the missing finger, is your mystery pen pal?"

Mac nodded.

"Do you remember that Clint Eastwood movie, The Good, The Bad, and The Ugly?"

She never ceased to surprise him. "Maybe. What about it?"

"The bad guy in that film was missing part of his finger."

"And...."

Rachel shook her head. "There is no 'and.' It just struck me that bad guys seem to be missing fingers."

Mac laughed again. Beautiful and full of trivia. He took another sip of coffee. He needed to focus.

He continued his list. "And twice, in as many days, somebody has tried to kill me."

Rachel put up her hand. "But we know, at least for the office attempt, that the shooter had all his fingers. So what does that mean?"

"Fingers or not, he's still a bad guy if he shoots a gun at me."

Rachel laughed. She stood up and opened the refrigerator, staring at the contents. "I can't think without food. How about pancakes and sausage?"

He was going to be fat when these bad guys, with all or none of their fingers, finally got to him.

"Sounds great. And if we don't get to go out on New Year's Eve, I promise we'll go some place soon where you can wear that new dress."

"It will keep. But at this rate, you won't." Rachel kept chatting as she began cooking. "Is it possible that somebody from your past, somebody you sent up the river…"

Mac raised an eyebrow.

"Down the river? Okay, you know what I mean, someone you sent to prison, is back and wants revenge?"

"Sure. Generally that happens more in movies than in real life, but it's possible. It just seems that all of this is related, but I don't see the connections yet."

Twenty minutes and a half-dozen legal pad sheets later, he was still no closer.

Rachel put a platter of pancakes and grilled sausages on the table. "Butter, syrup, or both?"

Mac found himself suddenly ravenously hungry. "Both, please."

Rachel refilled Mac's coffee cup and topped off hers. "Amanda Norman seems to be the key to the puzzle. I think you need to find Amanda Norman, or at least find out what happened to her. Maybe then, you can see the connections to all these bad guys."

Mac stopped chewing and made a note on the legal pad. "I think you're right. And the only person who seems to know Amanda, whether it's really her or an imposter, is her brother. I think I'll go out to the group home later this afternoon. I want to drop by the Police Station first and see if Greeley has anything for me."

Rachel nodded. "Sounds like a plan. I'll be ready to go about noon, after we both get a couple more hours sleep." She held up a hand to silence his objection. "I've got a few errands to run for the funeral home. As you know, death doesn't take weekends off. We'll go to see Lieutenant Greeley first, then take care of my list, and then we'll drive out to the group home. And before you start arguing with me, I want to make it clear that I am driving. You look like hell."

Mac started to protest, but he remembered what his face looked like in the bathroom mirror this morning. Black eyes and a swollen nose. Still…despite his injuries, he was a lone wolf. He didn't need a sidekick, except for maybe Whiskey.

"Forget it," she said, not even looking in his direction." You need my help."

Now she was reading his mind? Mac looked across the table at the curly-haired brunette digging into a stack of pancakes. He glanced down at his own plate and forked a sausage. Okay, no reason he couldn't have two sidekicks. Maybe he did need a driver. Just temporarily of course.

Chapter 9

"What in the Sam Hill happened?"

Edgar rolled off the elevator on his scooter, but pulled up short as he spied the yellow crime scene tape at the end of the hallway. The yellow plastic hung limply along the right edges of the office front door. Someone had too hurriedly affixed it and the side had come loose, no longer able to at least figuratively bar entry. Edgar dug out his office keys and scooted through the doorway to the front room. Chairs were overturned, papers were scattered on the floor. JJ's desk was on its side, a hole in the front panel.

Just then, he heard footsteps clomping up the stairs, footfalls that could only be made by hobnail boots.

He waited. He considered ducking for cover, but quickly realized there was no place safe to withstand the fury about to be unleashed.

But there was silence. Eerie silence as JJ walked into the offices of Sullivan Investigations, two rooms that she had single-handedly transformed into a professional suite through hard work and bargain-hunting trades.

Edgar watched as JJ lightly ran her fingers over the bullet hole in her desk. She checked the desktop computer, which someone had placed on the floor. The only sound the young assistant made was a small whimper when she found the jade plant that she had lovingly tended, broken, in pieces on the floor, dirt scattered across the oak planks that had been refinished a month earlier.

JJ walked to the coat closet, hung up her motorcycle jacket, and grabbed the broom. Methodically, she swept up the plant, shards of the clay flowerpot, and the dirt. She dumped it all unceremoniously into the garbage can, still without uttering a single word.

"Missy, you want to catch me up on what happened here? I had a message on my phone from Mac to come into the office this afternoon. Normally I don't work Sundays, but it sounded important. I get here and see this mess."

Edgar levered himself off the scooter and shuffled over to a chair. He gingerly sat down and looked expectantly at the young assistant. He couldn't decide if it was scarier to find Sullivan Investigations upended or deal with a silent JJ, face an impenetrable mask.

Still without a sound, JJ lifted the desk upright. For a slip of a girl, Edgar thought she was freakishly strong. Next came the computer, placed precisely in the center of the desk, the mouse to its right. He could hear her flip switches and the whir of the machine was familiar and soothing.

He was running out of patience.

"If you're not going to tell me, when will Mac be here? Did you know about this?"

JJ began typing, her fingers dancing across the keyboard. In a voice devoid of all emotion, not bothering to look at him, JJ explained, "Mac called me around midnight. Said there had been a shooting. He'll meet us here when he gets here. He wants us to find out everything we can about Hugo Alvira."

"Is he the one who did this? It's connected to that missing girl?"

Silence.

"JJ, is there some other case that would bring out the nutballs? One of those divorce cases you were all fired up for us to take? You know men who are catting around don't much appreciate being under surveillance Maybe one of them decided to…or maybe it was a wronged wife who decided to take her revenge…Missy, did Mac meet with one of those clients here last night?"

Other than the click of the keyboard, his questions were met with silence.

"Okay Missy, I've got my laptop. I'll be in Mac's office running searches on Mr. Alvira until somebody shows up who's willing to tell me what's going on. You don't have any reason to be so tight-lipped. You're as much a junior partner in this here operation as I am. Maybe more junior, seeing as how I've known Mac longer."

JJ stared at the senior citizen, shook her head and muttered. "You met Mac Sullivan one day before I did, old man. One day!"

Edgar had almost made it into Mac's office, the ten feet of shuffling taking its toll on the elderly man with emphysema. He stopped when JJ called after him.

"Wait a minute. I need you to do something."

Edgar turned slowly. He watched the assistant go to the office safe; swiftly turn the dial first one way, then the other, and then back again. She took out a large manila envelope, sealed with multiple layers of duct-taped. He'd seen it before, a few months earlier, when she had locked it in the safe.

She handed it to him. It wasn't heavy, but seemed full. Edgar shook it, but didn't hear much more than the contents moving around slightly.

"I need for you to keep this at your house."

"Why? You told me that it was the lease for this office, Mac's private detective license, and insurance papers."

JJ waved off his concerns. "It is, but after last night I don't think it's safe to keep here. What if the guy comes back? Burns the place down next time. You know all the paperwork Rachel's had to do for the funeral home fire? They lost a lot of records."

"Fine. Although I think you're getting paranoid for no good reason. Last night was probably just someone looking for drugs. Probably mixed up this office with the dentist's upstairs. Guy's been putting out flyers, might have attracted the wrong sort. Which reminds me, I left him a couple of messages about this temporary crown he put on me. I think it needs to be filed down a mite. He hasn't called me back."

"I haven't seen the dentist around lately, but you're right could be someone looking for drugs. Since he moved in there's been more traffic than usual in this building. I can hear people on the stairs at all hours." JJ shrugged. "But no use taking chances. You take this and put it somewhere in your house. Somewhere you can remember where it is, you hear me? Don't you dare lose it."

Edgar put the envelope in the shoulder bags attached to his scooter. "Don't get your panties all in a wad, Missy. I know how to keep things safe. You've got no idea what I've got hidden in my house."

"And don't give it to anyone except me, got it?"

Edgar was a little surprised at the intensity of JJ's voice. Low, fierce…and something else. "All this for some paperwork? What's really going on? Why not give it to Mac to safeguard?"

JJ went back to her desk and started typing again. "Mac's got enough going on without worrying about this stuff. My apartment building has had some break-ins or I'd take this home with me. This is our job to take care of stuff like this. Don't be bothering Mac with it. Understand."

"You're not the boss of me, Missy. Let's get that straight from the get-go. And I'm not buying your bullshit about this envelope, but I'll do what you want this time, cause I'm a nice guy and I figure you have Mac's best interests at heart. Just don't think for a minute, you've got me fooled. Something fishy is going on. When you're ready to talk to me, I'll listen."

"Fine. Whatever." JJ didn't bother to look up. "Mac won't be here for another couple of hours. Why don't you take that home now and do your research from there. I'll call you when Mac arrives."

He'd been dismissed. That much was clear. He didn't want to leave, but the urgency in her voice was coming through loud and clear. She wanted that package out of the office and she wanted it done quickly.

"You do that. Call me when Mac gets here. I've got some questions and he'd better have some answers. This is what you call, a hostile work environment, between you barking orders and bullets flying."

"If you don't like it…" JJ didn't finish her sentence.

Edgar's scooter was rolling through the doorway.

Chapter 10

Mac had a sick feeling in his stomach when he saw the whirring lights of the black-and-whites in front of the group home. There were four police cars, parked at angles to the curb. Evidence that there had been a rush to get inside.

Mac had his seat belt unbuckled before Rachel had pulled to a stop. "Stay here."

Rachel started to protest.

Mac shook his head. "I'll be lucky if they let me in. No way I can explain you or a dog sidekick. Keep Whiskey with you."

The big dog had been snoozing in the back seat of Rachel's Jeep, but perked up when she heard her name. She whined at being benched, but settled back down when Rachel offered a dog biscuit.

Mac got out of the car, every muscle in his body rebelling at moving with any kind of speed.

A uniformed cop, blocking the doorway, held up his hand. "Sorry sir, no one's allowed in."

Mac dug out his PI license. "I'm a retired DC cop. You can check with my old boss, Lieutenant James Greeley, homicide.

The cop lowered his hand.

Mac kept talking. "I've got my own investigations agency and I'm working on a case involving one of the residents. Can you at least tell Ms. Jackson that I'm here? I think I might be able to help."

129

Mac waited while the cop went inside. After a few minutes, he was ushered into the house and headed back to the big kitchen, passing the living room. He recognized some of the residents, huddled around the Christmas tree.

Melinda Jackson and what he assumed were two detectives sat at the long kitchen table. Three uniformed cops, talking on cell phones, stood in different corners of the room.

Ms. Jackson called out before Mac had even entered the room. "Randy's missing."

A wave of nausea hit him and he steadied himself against one of the counters before joining the group at the table.

A middle-aged, African-American detective stood up. "Hank Jefferson from the Arlington County PD." He tilted his head in the direction of the woman next to him. "My partner, Laura Mancino. I just checked with Greeley and he says you're legit, but to watch out for the dog. What the hell does that mean?"

Mac waved him off. "Nothing, Greeley has a thing about dog hair on his five hundred buck suits. Probably wants to save yours."

Jefferson, dressed in a plaid sports coat dating from the '80s, laughed. "What happened to you? You look like you lost a boxing match."

"Long story." Mac sat down across from Melinda Jackson. "What's going on here?"

Melinda Jackson nervously shredded a paper napkin. "I'm not sure, exactly. I had to run to the clinic in Annandale to pick up a prescription for one of the residents, but was sure I'd be back long before the mini-bus brought the men home from their field trip. They went to a professional basketball game in DC with some friends from the workshop. But an accident on Route 50 held me up and they were already waiting outside the door, except for Randy."

Mac tried to pin down a timeline. "Had he been on the bus with the others?"

Jackson tore the tiny pieces of the napkin into even smaller shreds that littered the kitchen tabletop. "I don't think so. The men seem a little confused, but Jose, who I can usually count on for accuracy...he works with Randy in Fairfax at the workshop. It's a place for developmentally disabled adults. Jose says that he didn't see Randy after they got to the game."

Jefferson checked his notes. "We've interviewed the chaperones and the bus driver. No clues there. We're trying to interview the staff at the workshop, but of course, they've off on Sundays. Supposedly an anonymous benefactor donated the Wizard tickets at the last minute. Sounds like a set up. I don't like it."

"Yeah. Me neither." But...something besides the tickets didn't add up. Mac thought for a moment, then asked, "You've got a lot of people on this case already. How come the big turnout of cops and cars?"

Jefferson exchanged looks with his partner. "Chief's son is one of the residents here."

Mac nodded, he certainly understood that explanation. Sometimes cases were very personal. This was one of them.

Mac turned to the group home manager. "Did Jose notice any strangers talking to Randy in the last couple of days? Have you seen anyone hanging around?"

Ms. Jackson nodded. "Jose said he saw a strange man talking to Randy on Friday. Drove a dark colored SUV. Of course, Jose might be off on time, but it seems unusual for Randy to be talking to anyone." She paused, then added, "Randy doesn't talk to strangers…you saw that for yourself the other day."

Mac checked with the detectives. "Was Jose able to give you a description?"

Laura Mancino checked her notes. "Very generic. Tall, white male, couldn't even describe his clothing."

"How tall?"

Mancino checked again. "Said very tall, if that means anything."

The nausea returned. Mac looked at the detectives. "Can I talk to Jose? I've got a question for him."

Mancino left the room and returned with a young man in his early 20s.

"Am I in trouble?" The young man searched Melinda Jackson's face. "I didn't know Randy would disappear."

The group home manager stood up and put her arms around Jose. "No, no. You're being a big help. Jose, this is Mac Sullivan. He's got a question for you."

Mac smiled at the young man. "Thanks for your help Jose. The man you saw talking to Randy. Was he wearing gloves?"

Jose looked confused, then brightened. "No, he wasn't wearing any gloves. His fingers were really cold I bet. It snowed. I always wear gloves when it snows."

Mac pushed a little. "Are you sure he didn't have gloves?"

Jose shook his head from side to side. "No gloves. No gloves." There was a pause, and then Jose added. "But his finger looked nasty. Part of it wasn't there. He should have worn gloves."

Jose stuck out his right hand and wriggled his ring finger to illustrate. He turned to Melinda Jackson. "Who is that guy? How does he know Randy?"

All eyes were on Mac.

Mac cleared his throat. "I think his name is Hugo Alvira. He is somehow connected to an old missing person's case that I've been investigating. I also think he tried to run me off the road a few nights ago. Alvira did time for burglary, suspected of worse. He's on parole."

Jefferson pulled out his phone and quickly connected to headquarters. He gave orders to put out an APB on Hugo Alvira.

Melinda Jackson started to walk out of the kitchen with Jose, when Mac stopped her. "Have the police gotten hold of Randy's sister?"

The group home manager shook her head. "No answer on the telephone number we have for Mandy. The police tried to trace it, but said they couldn't. I didn't understand why exactly, something about it being disposable. Maybe she got a new phone. Anyway, I don't have another way to reach her. I'm sure she'd be worried sick about her brother."

Mac wondered if this woman who claimed to be Amanda Norman really was the missing man's sister. She might be involved in the young man's abduction. Mac doubted that Randy would have gone anywhere with Alvira willingly. The whole situation was more complicated than he'd ever imagined.

Jefferson and Mancino prepared to leave. The male detective spoke briefly to the uniformed cops and then turned to Mac. "I'm going to leave a patrol car out front. Headquarters is emailing me an old headshot of this Alvira guy. We'll show it around, while we coordinate with DC authorities to look for him. I've got Randy's photo circulating too."

Mac headed for the front door. Several of the residents, including Jose, were staring out the front window, laughing and pointing. He opened the door and Whiskey came bounding in. The young men raced over to greet the hairy beast.

Jose got there first, fell to his knees, and was immediately smothered in dog kisses. "Whiskey, hey girl, so good to see you. You want some lasagna? I know you love lasagna. Or maybe we go to McDonald's? What do you say girl?"

Mac was stunned. How did the group know his dog?

Rachel ran in. "Sorry, sorry. I let Whiskey out to do her business and she ran straight for the house."

Mac crouched down so he was eye level with the group of residents fawning over Whiskey.

"How do you know Whiskey? Has she been here before?"

Jose stopped petting the dog for a moment. "Sure. Randy's sister brought her here a few weeks ago, and a couple of months before that."

Mac and Rachel exchanged glances. "Randy's sister brought this dog here?"

Melinda Jackson joined the group. "I've never seen this dog before, but I understood from Andrea that Mandy did have a dog. I think it must be the same one. Is that important? I'm sorry. I didn't realize....The residents talked about a large dog that Mandy brought to visit a couple of times. They seem to love her, especially Randy."

Nothing was making sense. Except Mac was pretty sure he'd found Amanda Norman.

***

The string of bells on the office door jangled for the last time. Mac ripped them from the doorframe and unceremoniously dumped them in the nearby fern planter.

JJ looked up from her keyboard in surprise. "Hey! What are you–"

"When you showed up here asking for a job, you knew who I was." Mac wasn't asking her, just making a statement. "You planned everything."

She met his stare without blinking.

It had taken him ten years but he'd solved the Amanda Norman case. He felt a little foolish. The missing girl had been working for

135

him for months and he'd been clueless. Some detective! He'd never run a background check on Julianna Jarrett. He'd always accepted that she was who'd she'd claimed to be.

"Amanda Norman in the flesh. What's the scam?"

"It's not a scam." JJ sighed. "Yes, after I met you at the college, I decided to....I knew you. Your name was in the early newspaper accounts of my disappearance. Later I was able to track you on-line. I've always known where you were. I thought–"

"What did you want from me? Did you send the postcards all these years? Or was it Hugo Alvira? Was it a game? Taunting me? Do you have any idea..." Mac crossed the front office space in three strides and stood in front of JJ's desk. "Or did you really want me to find you?"

"No." JJ swallowed hard. "I didn't send the postcards. I swear. I never knew about them, until you told me. Until you reopened the case. I never wanted anyone to find me. I left Amanda Norman back in that restroom in the Smithsonian. I became Julianna Jarrett that day and except for my brother, I never wanted to look back."

"Sure about that?" Mac leaned across the desk. "I can't believe a word you say. Don't even think about lying to me again, Amanda! It's over. What the hell were you doing all these years? Why did you run away in the first place? I met your foster parents, they were nice people."

"They were nice people, but they were strangers. They weren't my family. Randy was my family. For a long time I thought Uncle Hugo was...The point is that I didn't want to be Amanda anymore. I wanted to find my brother. I wanted to be free. I didn't send any postcards to you. Why would I want anyone to find me? I worked very hard at not being found."

"If you didn't send the postcards, you know who did."

She nodded. "I think it was Uncle Hugo."

"Looked like him on the surveillance tape? Why would he send postcards to me?"

"You have to understand that I didn't know about the postcards until this last one. When you told me about opening this cold case I was shocked. The last thing I wanted was for–"

"For me to find out the truth?" Mac slammed his hand on the desktop. "Why? Why were you still hiding?"

"I took some money from Uncle Hugo. It wasn't stealing exactly; my brother and I had earned most of it. I took it when he was thrown in jail and they removed us from his custody. They had been talking about splitting us up. I figured with the money, Randy and I could run away, find a place we could stay together. I was twelve. I didn't know that wasn't going to happen. They told me he was going to be in a special school, me...I was placed with a series of new foster parents. It seemed like every two months, I got moved again. By the time I got to the Millers, I had no idea how to find him."

"Why did you run away then? If you didn't know where your brother was, why leave then?"

"I saw Uncle Hugo parked in a truck outside the Miller house one day. He didn't see me, but I knew he had tracked me down. I had to leave. Uncle Hugo could be very good to people he liked, but if you crossed him, he got angry and stayed that way. A week after I saw him, the Miller house was broken into. Everyone thought it was just a random burglary, nothing much was taken. But I knew better. It was Uncle Hugo. He left me a note in my room. He warned me to give it back."

"The money?"

"That's what I thought then. I would have too, if I could have figured out how to get the money to him without getting close enough for him to grab me. I started seeing him everywhere. Looking back, I'm not sure how much was my imagination, how much was real. Two weeks after the break-in, I used the school trip to disappear. Thinking about it now, I can't believe he went to that much trouble for less than four thousand dollars."

"Some people kill for a lot less than that. Where'd you go? You were what? 14 when you ran away?"

JJ gave him a withering look. "It's not hard to get lost if you want to. Especially when you're nobody's kid and nobody really cares. Forged ID cards and Social Security cards are easy to get if you know where to look and are willing to pay."

"So you used the money you stole from Hugo...."

JJ sniffed. "Hey, I earned that money. He needed someone my size to crawl through basement windows when he was casing a joint. I earned every penny for all the scams I helped him pull off."

"What about Randy?"

"After I ran away it took me two years to find him. I paid someone to pull up his file," JJ answered, slamming a drawer shut and getting to her feet. "Two years. He thought I'd abandoned him. He thought I was dead. He still doesn't understand."

JJ pushed past Mac. "In case it's not obvious, I quit."

"Are you working with Hugo now? Do you know where Hugo took Randy? You may want to move on, but Randy seemed pretty happy at that group home. Don't destroy his life to protect your secrets."

JJ stopped dead in her tracks. Her face was so pale that Mac thought she might faint.

"What do you mean he took Randy? Why didn't Melinda call me?"

"You're not answering your cell phone. He's been missing for hours. One of the other residents, young guy named Jose, identified a tall man with a missing finger as the last stranger he saw talking with Randy."

"That son-of-a-bitch, I'll kill him."

"Come with me to the cops. Tell them what you know. They'll find Randy. They're looking for Hugo right now."

"You're off the hook." JJ started walking toward the door. "I'll handle it. I'll take care of myself and my brother just like I always have. And for God's sake, you don't have to feel guilty about Amanda Norman anymore. She's long dead."

"JJ...Amanda!" Mac grabbed her sleeve. "When you are ready to trust me, really trust me, give me a call. Otherwise, I have a business to get back to. And you can't quit, 'cause you're fired."

She jerked loose and ran towards the exit only to find Edgar and his scooter chair parked in the doorway.

The old man frowned. "What did I miss?"

Chapter 11

"It's been a long time, Uncle Hugo."

JJ had made it her business to learn where he was living. When Mac had told her he was meeting with Hugo Alvira, she had feared that Hugo would find her. She knew her best defense, if he got too close, was to become the aggressor.

She noted with some distaste that the house Hugo was currently residing in was much like the one he and his wife had owned back when she and Randy were living with them. Not too roomy, not too clean, not too safe. Speaking of safes, she'd lay money that Hugo had one hidden in a wall. If she had time after she found Randy, she'd look for it.

The back door had been open and she'd walked inside unannounced. She could see his feet, the footrest for the La-Z-Boy recliner in the air. The television was on. A movie airing. A musical.

That was her first clue that he might be dead.

Uncle Hugo had never willingly watched a musical in his lifetime.

JJ unzipped her leather jacket and unsnapped the flap on her shoulder holster. Over the last year, she'd spent many hours target shooting. She had no intention of being a victim ever again. She was an excellent shot. Unfortunately, or fortunately, however you looked at it, someone had stolen her thunder.

As she rounded the vinyl recliner, she saw the blood covering Hugo Alvira's shirt. He appeared to have been shot, but he wasn't dead. Not yet.

"Where's Randy?"

She pressed her Glock against the man's forehead, then changed her mind and pressed it against his left knee. She might have to ask her question several times, she'd save the headshot for last.

Hugo shook his head. "Not here. You shouldn't have taken them. I could forgive the money, but not....You knew what they meant to me. You had to know I'd never give up until I got them back. You brought this all on yourself. You always wanted more than people had to give."

"I have no idea what you are talking about. I don't care about anything now but finding my brother. Where is he?"

Hugo coughed, blood running down the side of his mouth, dripping on to the brown cushion. "Doc has him. You'll have to give him the coins. Trade the coins for Randy. Course Doc will still kill you both. He's in a real bad mood."

"I don't–"

The man coughed again, a gurgling sound coming from his chest. "Doc's been in a bad mood for the last thirty years."

"What coins? I don't have....Wait! Your pirate loot? The doubloons you stole from that museum? I didn't take them."

He stared at her. "Then you have no chance."

"Where is he? Where's Doc? Don't you dare die without telling...."

She watched the man's eyes roll back in his head. He began convulsing. She could have called 911.

She could have.

But she didn't.

***

"She's Amanda Norman?" Edgar asked for the umpteenth time. "I don't believe it."

"Believe it," Mac answered, staring out the window at the DC night. "I pulled her prints off that stapler on her desk. Greeley will get someone to check them against the Amanda Norman prints from that box of stuff left in the foster parents' attic. But it's her."

"So what are we going to do now?"

"Wait. We wait. I called those Arlington County detectives that are searching for Randell Norman. Told them everything I know. One of them, Jefferson, is coming by in a couple of hours to get a statement."

"And that's all you're going to do? The kid's out there on her own. I don't care how tough she thinks she is, she can't handle this alone."

"She lied to me. She lied to me over and over," Mac said. "If she wanted help from me she would have asked a long time ago."

"Oh, get over yourself." Edgar pulled out his cell phone and started punching in numbers. "This isn't about you right now. You can be pissed off later."

143

***

"Wait, where are you going?"

Rachel and Whiskey had just arrived at Mac's office building when they met him and Edgar on the way out.

"Ms. Brenner, we need to move. No lollygaggling with your sweetheart."

Rachel rolled her eyes. There was no point in trying to reason with Edgar.

"Mac, what's happening? Did you talk to JJ? What did she say?"

Mac had filled Rachel in during the car ride from the Group Home to his office. He'd asked her to take Whiskey to McDonald's for a snack so he could confront his assistant alone.

Mac grumbled, "Short story: She claims that she never sent me any postcards, knew who I was but didn't want to be found. Not that I believe that for a second, otherwise she wouldn't have taken the job here. She's played me for months and must have had a really good laugh when I reopened the case. Doesn't matter, she quit. Of course I fired her so we're pretty much even."

Edgar pulled on Mac's sleeve. "Time's a wasting and that kid ain't as smart as she thinks she is. Says she's going after this missing fingered Hugo guy by herself. Going to rescue her little brother like she was some kind of female Rambo. Now come on, we got to find her before she does something really stupid."

"I don't have to do anything. And she's already done something really stupid." Mac shook off Edgar's hand, but started to walk towards the old man's van anyway. The van was parked in the handicapped zone outside the building. Rachel followed.

As Edgar started to load his scooter, Mac turned to Rachel.

Rachel read his expression as a mixture of worry and anger. His relationship with JJ had been special and she wasn't sure how he was going to get past this revelation. She could tell he was reacting to JJ's on-going lie as a betrayal.

He rubbed the back of his neck. "Do me a favor?"

"Of course."

He handed her a key. "Take Whiskey and wait for me in my office. Lock the door. The Virginia PD is stopping by. Fill them in. If JJ comes back, convince her to stay there and call me."

"What are you going to do?"

He shook his head. "I have no idea."

***

The van sped off, Edgar at the wheel.

Whiskey whined, but Rachel pulled on her leash, moving her away from the curb. "Come on girl. We've been benched. But there's good news for you, I think JJ has some of those doggie treats you like in the mini-fridge."

Walking into the building, Rachel was pretty sure it was colder inside than out. Clearly Mac hadn't complained to the landlord about the lack of heat or maybe the landlord was selectively hard of hearing. She pulled on her gloves and envied Whiskey's thick coat.

The dog whined as a middle-aged, balding man came racing down the stairs, muttering profanities. Rachel quickly stepped out of the way. What little she could catch, she gathered he was dealing with a burst pipe in an upstairs bathroom.

"Excuse me, are you the landlord? Do you know that there's been no heat in this place–"

He man held up his hand to stop her. "Don't start. Furnace man was called last week. Finally showed up about an hour ago, should get some heat here soon, but I have to turn off the water before the whole place floods."

Rachel started up the stairs, as the man disappeared into the basement. She wondered, not for the first time, if Mac couldn't find a better, safer place for his business. Unlocking the office door, she flipped on the lights, and immediately locked the door again. She felt uneasy, like she should look in the closets for masked gunmen. Briefly she considered pushing the desk over to bar the door.

"Get a grip," she whispered. "Whiskey's obviously not worried."

The dog had wandered over to the mini-fridge in the corner of the room.

"Okay girl. You're on guard duty, so keep a sharp eye."

The dog snorted, then took the proffered treat and headed into Mac's office, settling down on the futon.

The clanking sounds emanating from the radiators told Rachel that the furnace was fixed. She nudged Whiskey slightly so she could share the futon and took out a worn paperback from her handbag. She pulled her coat tighter and opened the book.

"So now we wait."

Two things woke her up. First, was a pounding on the office door; the second, the sauna-like atmosphere in the room. Clearly the furnace was working again. Maybe too well.

"Sullivan, you in there? Arlington PD, open up."

Whiskey, who had fallen asleep as well, was snuggled up close, and whined as Rachel struggled to her feet. She checked her watch. She'd been sleeping for close to an hour.

She pulled open the door and recognized the two detectives who had been at the Group Home.

Laura Mancino was holding her winter scarf up to her face.

Hank Jefferson, who had pulled his jacket over his nose, pushed his way into the office. "Where's Sullivan?"

Rachel started to gag. "What's ...Oh my God, that smell. Where's it coming from?"

Whiskey had wandered into the front room and immediately started ferociously barking. The dog dashed out the door and headed up the stairway.

Rachel and the detectives followed after her. The dog raced to the third floor and then down the hall. She stopped in front of an office door and started to howl.

Rachel recognized the stench as she got near. She'd worked in funeral homes long enough to recognize the sweet, sickly, overwhelming odor of a rotting body.

She grabbed Whiskey's collar and pulled her back from the door. Running her hand through the dog's thick coat, she sought to reassure her. "Hush, girl. We know, we know."

The two detectives exchanged glances. They pounded on the door of Dr. Felix Payne, D.D.S. When there was no answer, Jefferson kicked in the door and he and Mancino entered the dentist's office. Rachel stayed back in the hall, holding tightly to an excited dog.

She heard Mancino yell, "All clear."

In a few minutes, the two came out. Jefferson was on his phone. "Yeah, multiple gunshot wounds. Body placed next to the radiator so time of death is unclear. He kind of looks like a cooked hot dog on a spit. Doesn't smell like one though."

Mancino looked up, meeting Rachel's gaze. "Sorry. My partner is kind of...." She coughed into her scarf. "I'll never get used to that smell."

"Is it Dr. Payne?" Rachel asked. Whiskey had settled down, still glued to Rachel's side, but finally quiet.

"You know him?" Jefferson asked. "DC Police will be here in a couple of minutes. Homicide squad, judging from the bullet wounds. I've opened some windows; see if we can dissipate the smell."

Rachel shook her head. "Poor man. I talked to him briefly. Told me he had just opened his office. This place is a death trap. Someone shot at Mac a day ago. Now Dr. Payne. Maybe it's the same guy. Probably looking for drugs, don't you think?"

"Someone shot at Sullivan? Here?"

Rachel nodded. "Mac's not sure who or why. He thought it might be connected to the Amanda Norman case, but now that Dr. Payne is dead....Maybe there's something else happening here."

She could hear the sirens coming closer. Leaning back against the wall, she released her hold on Whiskey. Surprisingly the big dog ran into the office.

"Get that dog out of the crime scene." Jefferson yelled.

"Whiskey, come here, come here." Rachel ran into the office and found the dog howling over the bloodied body. Multiple gunshot wounds riddled the victim's chest.

Rachel grabbed Whiskey's collar and dragged the dog out of the office.

Jefferson pulled the door closed. "Put that dog away before Homicide gets here."

Rachel held a frustrated Whiskey tight, the big dog continuing to protest. "That's not Dr. Payne. Who do you think it is? "

Jefferson and Mancino exchanged glances. "According to the vic's driver's license and some flyers around the office, that's Dr. Felix Payne. Photos match."

"No. The man who introduced himself as Dr. Payne didn't look like that. He was older, a little rough around the edges. I thought he looked like the type of dentist who would open an office in this building. The dead guy isn't the same person."

"Are you sure? The decomp can–"

"I work in a funeral home. I'm sure."

"So the man Ms. Brenner met may be our killer," Jefferson said, giving a nod to Mancino. He turned back to Rachel. "Tell us about your encounter."

"It was just yesterday." She pointed towards the dentist office. "The guy in there has been dead longer than that. The man I met told me that he had just moved into the building…that he had noticed that a private detective also had offices here. He asked me about Mac's hours, whether he had an assistant…." She looked at the two detectives. "I thought he wanted to make an appointment."

Mancino shrugged. "He's probably been casing Sullivan's office. Are we sure that his assistant is that missing teenager?"

Jefferson checked his notes. "Sullivan said he'd dropped off some of the teen's items for fingerprinting with Lt. Greeley downtown. He also said he'd pulled prints from something on his assistant's desk. But since Sullivan's not on the force anymore, we'll pick up another set of prints here of what's her name…Julianna Jarrett. Make it official. The DC police can probably have a definitive answer in a couple of hours."

"Mac said she admitted…." Rachel could hear the sound of footsteps coming up the stairs. The cavalry had just arrived.

Jefferson and Mancino walked over to the stairwell.

Rachel took one last look at the doorway to the dentist's office and decided her presence was no longer needed. "Come on girl."

Rachel tugged at Whiskey, urging her towards the staircase. "Let's go back down to the office and call Mac."

She couldn't figure out why the Amanda Norman case was triggering all these deaths. Or rather why the current investigation of the case was stirring up all this violence. Was the faux dentist the killer? What about Hugo Alvira? How did he fit into the puzzle? And JJ? Oh, lord what was going on with that girl?

"I should have tried to get to know her better," Rachel mused, pausing to look at the lettering on the front of the Sullivan Investigations office door. She remembered Mac telling her how JJ had done the lettering herself. The girl had put so much effort in to decorating the office, trying to help get the business in the black.

"She was just trying to make a place for herself, trying to be important to someone," Rachel said, stroking the dog's head. "Don't worry, Mac will figure that out eventually."

Whiskey whined and as though understanding what was happening, walked over to JJ's desk and sat down in front of it.

Chapter 12

"Edgar, I thought we were going downtown to talk with Greeley. You missed the turn."

"We need to stop by my house first. I've got something there you should see."

Mac stared out the passenger window, trying to process the day's events. He was second guessing every conversation he'd ever had with JJ or rather Amanda. Why had she ingratiated herself into his life? She must have had a reason, but for the life of him he couldn't figure it out. She was never who he thought she was.

"Fine." Mac shifted uncomfortably in his seat. He didn't have the energy to continue arguing with Edgar. The old man and JJ had never gotten along, but ironically he was much more accepting of the girl's deception than Mac was.

"I'd never planned on being responsible for so many people," Mac said. He hadn't realized he'd said the words aloud until Edgar responded.

"We make plans and then life happens and those plans dissolve like cheap toilet paper," Edgar said. "I spent my life working sixty hours a week so that I could retire with my wife and enjoy the good things in life. Then once I retired, I got sick, my wife died, and I realized that the "good things" in life weren't what I thought they were. I'll give you the benefit of my experience – people are the good things. Me, you, JJ, we're pretty much family now. None of us had anyone one else in our lives until you came along. Maybe you never made the decision to create this little family of ours. But it is, what it is. JJ needs our help whether she wants it or not. And we need to give it whether we want to or not."

"Explain to me your relationship with JJ. I thought you couldn't stand each other."

Edgar chuckled. "Sibling rivalry? Seriously, though. JJ and I understand each other. If you think about it, what could be more important than having someone in your life who cares enough to argue with you?"

Mac didn't respond. He wasn't sure what he was feeling.

Edgar turned the van into his driveway. "Don't remember leaving a light on."

Mac stared at the house. The two-story house was dark except for a light glowing in an upstairs window. As he watched, the light bobbed up and down, then disappeared. "It's someone with a flashlight."

"You think it's that Alvira fellow? The one with the missing finger who sent you those postcards?"

"Who knows? Normally, I'd say you just have a burglar, but this is one too many coincidences. Call 9-1-1. Then move your van down the block."

"Sure thing." Edgar punched in the number on his cell phone, and put the van into reverse, hesitating when Mac unfastened his seatbelt and opened the van door. "What are you doing?"

Mac showed him his handgun. "I'm tired of being used for target practice. I'm going hunting. "

***

Lt. Greeley told her to go home and take Whiskey with her, that he'd make sure the office was locked before he left the scene. The CSI technician was through with her, Mac's office, and Whiskey. The technician had taken a sample of Whiskey's fur. She'd taken Rachel's fingerprints for elimination purposes. She'd also dusted around JJ's desk and computer for the girl's fingerprints.

Rachel glanced in her rearview mirror. An officer she'd met a few times before, Detective Pete Fiori, was following her home. Lt. Greeley had told the former undercover narcotics officer to stay with her until they figured out who might be next in the killer's playbook. Rachel was glad of the protection but not happy with having a relative stranger living with her. If she remembered correctly, the middle-aged, but younger looking Detective Fiori hardly spoke and had problems with crowds. Mac had mentioned that although an excellent cop, the man had a work-related phobia involving being around lots of people in confined spaces. Detective Fiori might not appreciate her house. Although she lived alone, lately she'd never managed to actually be alone there. Of course there was another option. Lt. Greeley had suggested that now would be a great time for her to leave town on an extended trip. The problem was she had nowhere to go. No place else she wanted to be. And frankly, she couldn't afford to leave town. So it appeared she was going to get to know Detective Fiori very well.

Arriving at her house, she was surprised to find Edgar's van parked in front, the old man standing by the driver's door, his face turned towards his own home down the street.

She jumped out of her Jeep, leaving a sleeping Whiskey keeping the backseat warm.

"Edgar? What's going on?"

"Got a burglar in my house. Mac's in there alone. I called 9-1-1 but who knows how long it will take to get someone here."

Detective Fiori arrived in time to catch most of what Edgar had relayed. "Which house? Anyone else supposed to be in there? Do you have any weapons on the premises?"

Rachel watched with Edgar as Detective Fiori radioed in his situation and ran down the block to Edgar's house.

She was beyond being worried. She was exhausted with all the drama in her life. "What else can go wrong?"

Edgar just looked at her. "Plenty."

***

The house was dark. Mac slipped down the driveway to the back porch. The door was unlocked. He noticed that a small basement window had been pried open. Standard operating procedure for a burglar–break-in through the basement, but unlock a door for quick escape.

He slowly pushed the door open, hoping that Edgar had recently oiled the hinges. He had. Once inside the kitchen, Mac could hear someone moving in a room above him. Light, scurrying feet, moving from point-to-point. He could hear drawers being opened and closed. Someone was looking for something specific. This wasn't a snatch-and-grab heist.

Mac edged into the dining room, staying close to the wall, his gun in his right hand, ready to duck, cover, and if necessary, fire. But the noises upstairs continued, as the person moved across the hall into another room.

Suddenly, he heard the back door open.

"Damn, I told her to stay put." Sure that Rachel had come to help, despite his warnings, Mac moved quickly back towards the kitchen. There, in the shadows, he saw a male figure, move lightly across the floor, alert, with both hands on his gun, in a stance Mac instantly recognized as the product of Police Academy training.

"Sullivan?" It was barely a whisper, but Mac knew the voice.

He answered. "Fiori? Perp is on the second floor. May be armed."

They began the familiar dance of move, pause, check, move again, until they were in the living room, the stairs to the second floor ahead. They pressed themselves against the far wall, as the intruder started down the steps. Fiori cocked his head toward a lamp and nodded. Mac knew what to do. Flip the switch as soon as the suspect hit the bottom step.

Just as light flooded the room, Fiori yelled. "Freeze. This is the police. Put your hands where I can see them."

Mac was stunned. Before he could say anything, the burglar started to run to the back door.

Fiori shouted, "Stop or I'll shoot."

Mac took off and got between the cop and the suspect. "JJ, don't be an idiot."

The young woman was almost at the door when she slipped slightly on the kitchen linoleum. It gave Mac just enough time to tackle her.

JJ fought like a wildcat, and Mac could feel her about to flip him on his back, like an upended turtle. Finally Fiori waded in, snatched the girl's wrists, snapped on cuffs, and hauled her to her feet.

"Let me go, you bastard, let me go." JJ tried to kick Fiori, but Mac grabbed her and pulled her back against him.

Mac growled, "Don't be stupid and get yourself arrested for assaulting a police officer."

"You know her?"

Mac nodded, still struggling to hold JJ in place. "She's my assistant."

"Former assistant! I quit, if you remember, old man."

Mac, for a change, agreed with her. He was old. "I fired you, but for current purposes, you're still in my employ. So shut up and behave!"

DC uniformed cops swarmed into the kitchen, followed by Rachel, Edgar, holding fast to her arm, and a very excited Whiskey. The senior citizen was breathing so heavily that Mac feared the toll all the excitement was taking on him. Edgar was too winded to talk and sank down on a kitchen chair.

"JJ, thank God, you're okay."

Mac could trust Rachel to take the maternal point of view. He was slightly irritated that she didn't even ask how he was. "She's fine now, but if she kicks me one more time…"

"What are you going to do, old man?"

Edgar struggled to his feet, his voice wheezing, but clear. He addressed the uniform cops. "There's been a terrible mistake, officer. I didn't know my great-niece was in the house. I weren't expecting her. There hasn't been a break-in. I'm sorry for your trouble."

Fiori and Mac exchanged glances. For a change, even JJ was silent.

"Are you sure, sir?"

Edgar nodded, and then sat back down. He motioned to Rachel, who listened to his whisper, then scurried into the living room. In a moment she was back with an oxygen canister. Edgar shakily attached the oxygen with a nasal cannula. His breathing started to smooth out.

After Fiori removed JJ's handcuffs, he filled Mac in on the latest homicide. Mac was too stunned to ask any questions. He walked Fiori and the other DC officers to the front door. The uniformed cops headed back to their patrol cars. Fiori was still assigned as protective detail for Rachel and Edgar.

Mac shook Fiori's hand. "Thanks for the backup, You're a good man to have in a bad situation."

Fiori snorted. "You want to tell me what the hell is going on? I know that's not really his great-niece."

Mac smiled. "No, she's not. But Edgar would tell you that we're one big, dysfunctional family. You going to park outside the house, circle around periodically?"

The detective nodded. "My partner is on her way. With two houses to cover I'm going to need some help. Lt. Greeley may send me another officer to assist but with budget cuts–"

"Let me see if I can get to the bottom of this, find out what JJ knows or doesn't know about her brother's disappearance and if it has anything to do with the murder of the dentist. I suspect it does, but I'll be damned if I know what."

Fiori headed out. "I'll check in with headquarters to see if they have an update on...on any of it."

Mac headed back to the kitchen. If this is what it means to have a family, was it any wonder that he was a confirmed bachelor?

Chapter 13

"Give me the gun." Mac held out his hand to JJ. "You're just lucky that Fiori didn't know you had a firearm on you. No way he wouldn't have arrested you on the spot."

JJ didn't flinch. "You're going to have to pry it out of my cold dead fingers."

"That could be arranged," Mac warned. "I've about had enough of your attitude."

Whiskey whined and brushed against the young woman.

Rachel was at the stove heating water for tea. "What gun? JJ, you have a gun?"

The young woman rolled her eyes. "Not everybody leads a charmed life, Mrs. Brenner. I'm just taking care of me and my brother every way I know."

Edgar who had been quietly watch the conversation unfold, his breathing smoother, but still ragged, levered himself shakily up from his chair.

"Watch your mouth, Missy. These folks ain't done nothing but try to help you, whether you're smart enough to know it or not. Now if you'll listen instead of going off half-cocked, Mac will figure out how to find your brother and get this here killer off your case. Then you can go anywhere you want. But right now, give Mac the gun."

"I didn't ask for help. If you'd all get out of my way, I'd take care of myself and Randy. Always have, always will."

Mac patience was gone. "Listen. Your damn privacy has meant that somebody's trying to kill anyone who gets in between him and whatever it is that you have that he wants. Stop acting like this is all about you. Trust me, at this point, this killer's got no compunction about knocking off any one of us who gets in his way."

JJ glared at three people in the room, then slowly reached under her coat, drew the gun from its holster, and handed it to Mac.

Rachel brought over steaming mugs of tea to the table and motioned for everyone to sit down. Reluctantly, JJ and Mac took chairs across from each other.

"I still have some of that coffee cake you made for Christmas in the bread box, Ms. Brenner, if you want to put it out." Edgar started coughing and reached for his mug of tea. "A little food might settle everyone's nerves. Can't believe my new dentist is dead. Guess it's back to the yellow pages."

Whiskey looked up expectantly. Rachel brought over a bowl of water and a slice of the cake. She put the rest of the cake on a plate for the group.

JJ frowned. "Dentist? What are you talking about, old man?"

Mac held up a hand. "Later, JJ. First I want you to do some talking."

There were a few moments of silence, broken only when JJ said softly, "Okay. I should probably mention first that Hugo Alvira is dead."

Mac caught JJ's eyes and without words, asked the question.

"I didn't kill him. I would have," she added fiercely, "but he was already dying when I got there. Randy wasn't there, but he admitted he'd taken him."

Rachel reached across and grabbed JJ's hand. "Start at the beginning, or at least the beginning of tonight."

JJ took a deep breath. "I knew where Uncle Hugo lived. Like I told Mac, I did take money from Hugo all those years ago, but it wasn't stealing. I earned it. I needed to make sure that Randy and I could always start over, someplace new."

Mac nodded for her to continue.

"When I got to Uncle Hugo's tonight, he was…he was about out of time. Told me that Doc had shot him. Hugo mentioned a double cross. Apparently Hugo had seen me going in and out of your office. They've been watching the office, following you around." She sighed. "Anyway, he recognized me. But he didn't tell Doc right away, so they had a fight when Doc found out. Hugo lost. Hugo always lost when he got involved with him. The bastards kidnapped Randy. But...they never could work together long without arguing. Hugo didn't get any pleasure from hurting people. Oh, he'd do it, but he wouldn't enjoy it. Doc was different. I think he killed Louise Miller."

Mac stopped her. "Did he say where Randy is now?"

"No. All he said was that Doc had taken Randy and was going to use him to get the coins back from me. But I don't have Hugo's coins. I've never had them. The only thing I ever took from Hugo was the cash. Like I said, I earned every single one of those dollars."

Mac pushed back his chair and started pacing. He thought better when he moved, although with all the pummeling his body had taken recently, he felt every muscle rebel with each step. Whiskey followed him, nudging at his leg, pushing him back towards the chair.

"Let's start with the basics. Who's Doc?"

JJ spread her hands out on the table, and then balled them into fists. "Doc is Hugo's brother. I don't know his real name. He was around some of the time when I was living with Hugo and his wife, but she didn't like him, thought he got Hugo in trouble, so he wasn't welcome at their house. I think they called him Doc because he was good at impersonating doctors when they were pulling scams."

Rachel held up a hand. "Think he'd pretend to be a dentist?"

JJ shrugged. "Sure, maybe. Why?"

Mac's aching body, and Whiskey's constant insistence, forced him to sit back down. "Rachel and Whiskey discovered a dead body in the offices of Dr. Felix Payne."

Edgar looked up and sighed. "Hopefully the real dentist fixed my tooth, not the fake one."

Rachel pushed the last piece of coffee cake towards the elderly man. Color had begun to return to his cheeks. "That's what the police say based on his driver's license and some flyers they found in the office. But he's not the same man who introduced himself to me as Dr. Payne so now I'm thinking that the imposter was–"

"Doc, casing the joint and looking for me," JJ finished.

Mac took a sip of his tea. He wished it were Scotch, but he'd have to wait on that. "What coins is this Doc guy looking for?"

"Pirate treasure that Uncle Hugo stole from a museum decades ago. Spanish doubloons. He always thought they were special. Wouldn't let us near them."

JJ rubbed her eyes and for a moment, looked younger. Mac glanced at the clock. He couldn't remember the last time he slept. Looking at the others at the table, he was pretty sure none of them had any shut-eye recently. Even Whiskey was snoring lightly at his feet.

"Okay, this is what we're going to do. Everyone's going to sleep for a couple of hours and we'll start fresh in the morning."

JJ stood up, brushing away unwanted tears. "No way. Randy's out there. I've got to keep looking for him. He's scared and confused. He can get whiny…kid-like when he's scared…Doc doesn't care. He just killed his own brother. You think he cares about mine?"

Rachel put her arms around the young woman. "Listen to me. Doc's not going to hurt your brother until he's of no value to him anymore. Right now, Randy is his best bargaining chip. He knows you're going to want to see Randy before you hand over these coins he thinks you have. I'm not saying he won't try and kill you both once he has them, but Mac's not going to let that happen. None of us will. Right now, let's get a couple of hours sleep and start fresh."

"This is how it's going to work," Mac announced.

The group looked at him.

"We need to stay together. It will be easier for the cops to offer protection and for me to make sure that nothing happens if we're all under one roof. Rachel, okay if we use your house?"

"Of course."

Edgar shook his head. "That's not going to work for me. Too many steps and I need my oxygen when I'm sleeping. You all go on over. I'll be fine."

Mac thought a moment. "No. I want everyone in one place. You go to bed and we'll all camp out on the floor in the living room."

Edgar got to his feet. "No need for that. There's two extra bedrooms and a bath up on the second floor. Ms. Brenner and JJ can take them. Unless you want to share one of them." The old man winked, but it lost some of its punch when he started coughing.

Rachel handed him his mug and Edgar took a sip.

The group headed for the living room. Edgar shuffled over to a closet and brought out a pillow and a wool blanket and handed them to Mac. "Take the couch. It's not bad for sleeping."

JJ started up the steps, then turned and asked. "Who used to stay in the little girl's room? I saw it when I was…"

She stopped, embarrassed to admit that she had broken into Edgar's house.

The old man was silent, looked at a frame, on the mantelpiece, that held a photo of a laughing young girl. Finally he said softly. "My daughter. She was killed when she was nine. Drunk driver. My wife was never the same. Guess neither of us was."

He headed towards his room, but JJ's voice cut across the silence.

"What was her name?"

Edgar didn't look back. His answer was barely a whisper. "Amanda."

Chapter 14

The radio chatter between the four vehicle convoy was not reassuring. Mac, Edgar, JJ, and Rachel were riding in Edgar's van. Detective Pete Fiori and his partner Joanna Giles were trailing the van in a police cruiser. The two cops from Arlington County, Hank Jefferson and Laura Mancino were in a police SUV in front of Mac. Two state troopers from the Virginia State police were riding point. They were headed in a convoy to a cabin in West Virginia, owned by Raoul Alvira, aka Doc. The area was a haven for paramilitary groups; guns and ammo not only welcome, but expected. There were no guarantees that Doc and Randy would be there, but from what could be gleaned from undercover police contacts in the area, it was the perfect hideout, with no neighbors close by or likely to butt in.

Mac would have liked to have checked out the area on his own, but the police wouldn't hear of it. This case was getting more and more complex.

"Can't believe you put a police radio in your van," JJ said. "How much did that set you back?"

"Never you mind Missy. My great-nephew got me a deal on it. If we'd had more time, I would have called him to come with us."

Mac held up a hand. "Everyone be quiet, I need to listen. Edgar, they are switching channels, can you–"

"Got it."

"Now everyone shut up."

***

The radio traffic increased as they got closer to their destination.

"Anyone know where we are? Jefferson? Sullivan?"

"Virginia still, I think. Just keep following those Virginia Troopers."

"Nah, I think we're probably in West Virginia by now."

"This is Sullivan. We passed a sign. Did anyone read it?"

"Jefferson here. Hard to tell with this snow blowing sideways now. Fiori, get your partner to check the GPS reading again. We need to get one of those that actually works. Mancino make a note."

"Sullivan talking. Do we have anyone with us with jurisdiction in West Virginia?"

"I'll make a call. Get some assistance from the Feds."

"Fiori. Are you sure about that Jefferson? Myself I'd rather have a root canal than deal with the FBI."

"Joanna Giles. I'm not getting a cell signal? Anybody?"

"I've got two bars. Who should I call?"

"Fiori talking. Lt. Greeley will have an FBI contact. Call him."

"Know anyone in the West Virginia State Police?"

"What's the range on this radio Mancino? All I'm getting is static. Can anyone hear me?"

"Fiori talking. Give me five minutes before you involve the Feds. I'll call Captain Jim Bellman at their headquarters in South

Charleston. My partner says she met him at one of those mandated law enforcement seminars."

"We'll probably need the FBI anyway. Lot of federal parks in the area."

"Mancino here. Forget the FBI. We might need State Park Rangers. Do they have bears in West Virginia?"

"Hibernating now."

"I heard that with global warming, they don't sleep well anymore."

"No one sleeps well anymore. Too much caffeine."

"Who's talking?"

"Joanna Giles. I don't like wildlife. How much longer?"

"If you don't like wildlife, how did you get partnered up with Fiori? You don't have to worry about bears being out today. Must be topping out at 10 degrees."

"Sullivan here. The kid doesn't have gloves. Not much of a coat."

"Kidnapper will take care of him until he's got the ransom. And I was only wild in my younger years. Fiori out."

"Oh, hell. Go ahead. Call the FBI. Let's get everybody on board. Make it a real party."

***

Mac glanced at Rachel and JJ in the back seat. The chatter wasn't reassuring. Again he wished they could have made this trek alone with the DC detectives.

"Too many cooks in the kitchen," Rachel said, her words mirroring his thoughts.

He shifted his gaze to JJ. The young woman had been staring out the window for the last hour without making any comment.

"JJ, are you ready to tell us why you broke into Edgar's house? Seems to me you never did explain that," Mac asked.

Edgar cleared his throat. "I think she was looking for a package she asked me to take home for safekeeping."

JJ continued to direct her attention at the passing scenery.

"JJ," Rachel urged, "It's time to tell us everything. We only want to help."

"That envelope doesn't have anything to do with what Doc wants. It has my emergency money, a couple of fake ids for me and Randy, my bankbook, and keys to an old car I have stored in a garage in Warrenton. I was afraid to keep it at the office after the shooting."

"Warrenton?" Rachel asked in surprise. "My Warrenton? Why would you keep a car that far away?"

Mac took his eyes from the road long enough to catch JJ's gaze as she turned from the window to answer Rachel.

Red-faced, JJ crossed her arms and shrugged.

"Buses go to Warrenton. She was going to hide out there like your brother did. At the Thayer Farm," Mac guessed. "Doc got to Randy before you could, didn't he, Amanda?"

"Don't call me that," JJ exclaimed. "Amanda was weak. She was scared out of her mind half the time. I'm not her. Not anymore."

"I don't know about that," Edgar interjected. "You're still scared. Your first instinct is still to run away, instead of depend on the people who love you."

JJ narrowed her eyes and glared at Edgar. "Just where did you hide my money anyway, old man? I'm gonna get that back, you know. Don't you think I won't."

Edgar cackled. "I hid it good, didn't I, Missy. You wanted it safe. It's safe."

"You looked in it, didn't you?" JJ said, a frown seemingly permanently etched on her face.

Edgar smiled. "Course I did."

***

"Snowstorm is turning into a blizzard," Mac said. "We're going to have to move fast if we're going in tonight."

Law enforcement had set up a command post about five miles from the location of Doc Alvira's cabin. Planes were grounded, so the group was limited to the convoy from DC and a dozen or so West Virginia State Troopers. The FBI was still en route.

"Explain why you believe the kidnap victim Randell Norman is being held in this cabin?"

The person asking the question was the West Virginia Captain who'd assumed leadership of the entire operation. Mac supposed someone needed to be in charge and it might as well be West Virginia since that's where they were, if not where the cabin was. The actual cabin location was so close to the line that if the structure

173

ended up having more than one room, some of them might be located in Virginia. Jurisdiction could be tricky if someone got killed in the raid.

Mac watched as Pete Fiori nodded at his partner, Detective Joanna Giles. She was technically Fiori's superior officer although the only time he acknowledged it was in situations like this. He didn't like speaking in front of a group and left that role to her.

Detective Giles stepped to the front. Forty-something, single, with short dark hair, and piercing blue eyes, she was known for her no-nonsense attitude and sharpshooter skills. Mac hoped this rescue wouldn't need her special sniper talents, but Doc Alvira was a wild card. The man hadn't contacted JJ yet to arrange a ransom. Bringing Randy to the middle of nowhere didn't make a whole lot of sense to Mac, but he had to assume the kidnapper had a plan worked out. The group was well aware that they could be walking into an ambush.

Looking at her notes, Detective Giles said, "Randell Norman is a 22-year-old, white male, with some mental impairment due to fetal alcohol syndrome. He is considered a critical missing. He was seen at a Wizards basketball game at the Verizon Center in DC. We believe he was in the company of a man fitting the description of Hugo Alvira."

"The missing finger guy? The dead one?" Arlington County Detective Laura Mancino asked.

"Only one missing finger guy and he's very dead."

"One finger or one guy?" a West Virginia trooper joked.

"Shut up, Wheeler. How is Hugo Alvira connected to this cabin we're going to?" another trooper asked.

"He's not, but his brother is. We researched land records for Hugo Alvira and his extended family members for Virginia and the surrounding states. His maternal grandfather owned 200 acres of this mountainside. The deed had been transferred to one Raoul Alvira aka "Doc" about 20 years ago. Raoul Alvira is Hugo Alvira's brother. Doc has been implicated in more than a dozen burglaries and almost as many assaults. He was convicted of two lesser charges early in his career, served less than three years in prison. Some cons get religion in prison, some just get an advanced criminal education. Doc Alvira got the education. After prison he continued his string of crimes, but never left another living witness. He's a suspect in three older murders in Virginia and three recent ones in the DC area. We believe he murdered his brother Hugo Alvira yesterday. One gunshot to the chest.

"Families aren't what they used to be," Edgar grumbled.

Detective Giles gave the old man a quick look. Almost none of the law enforcement group was happy with Mac's associates being included in the operation. They were there on limited suffrage and Edgar just used up one of his chips.

Mac clapped one hand on Edgar's shoulder and nodded at Detective Giles.

Mollified, Detective Giles said, "The second murder victim was one Dr. Felix Payne. Dentist. Another gunshot to the chest. Time of death is debatable. Because of low temperatures in the dentist office, he might have been dead as long as four days."

Giles paused expecting decaying dentist jokes. When none were forthcoming she continued. "The third murder victim was Louise Miller, fifty-something housewife. She was living in the house where Randell's sister, Amanda Norman, had been a foster child. Ballistics were a match. Time of death was approximately three days ago. Same gun was used in all three shootings. A search of the dentist's office revealed a pair of bloodied Miami Dolphins team gloves stuffed behind the radiator near the body. The men living in the group home where Randell Norman resides all had matching Dolphin gloves given to them by the father of one of the group home residents. Apparently the father is a big Miami Dolphin fan. The blood on the gloves is the same type as Randell's. There were some drugs missing. We're guessing the brothers might have used the drugs to help keep Randell under control."

"That still doesn't get us to West Virginia," the West Virginia Captain said. "The dentist was killed before the young man was kidnapped. You think they brought the kid back to the dentist's office for a visit? With the body still there?"

Giles nodded. "That's our working theory. We think they waited there. That they intended to confront Amanda Norman in the Sullivan Investigation office one floor down from the dentist's. For some reason that didn't work out. I suspect the dog being in and out of the Sullivan office was a factor. Or maybe Amanda wasn't there when they were. But we know from the bloody gloves that Randell

Norman was in the dentist office at some point after the dentist was injured."

"What makes you think this Doc Alvira and Randell Norman are in West Virginia now?"

Detective Hank Jefferson waved his hand, indicating he'd answer that one. "Doc used one of Louise Miller's credit cards and the DC police had a flag on it. Video from the convenience store showed Doc and Randell paying for gas and buying food and drink. The store was the one we passed about 30 miles back. They've got to be coming here."

Mac stepped forward then. "That's enough background. Now let's talk about how we're going to get that boy out alive."

***

"I can't believe they expect me to wait here while they raid the cabin," JJ complained, pacing back and forth outside Edgar's van.

Rachel shut the door, giving up on getting JJ back in the van. Sitting inside with Edgar and Whiskey, with the heater blowing, Rachel noted that the young woman was wading in knee-deep snow drifts now, the icy substance severely restricting her movements. Rachel wondered how the law enforcement team was faring as they approached the cabin. The decision had been made to drive no closer than a half mile and walk in. They were going to park their vehicles below a hill that protected them and the cabin from view. That protection came at a cost. They would have to withstand the uphill trek through the deep snow, virtually sitting ducks if Doc Alvira happened to crest the hill and look down.

One of the West Virginia State Troopers had been left behind to man the radio and provide some security for the civilians. Glancing over at the young officer in his patrol car, drumming his fingers on the steering wheel, she could see he and JJ shared a common frustration at being left out of the action.

"It's only been 20 minutes," Edgar said. "They're still walking up the hill. She needs to settle down. Young people don't know how to deal with waiting. It's not easy for anyone, but it's a necessary skill to learn if you want to survive in this world."

"I'm not that good at waiting, myself," Rachel admitted. She was getting increasingly unhappy with the role she seemed to have fallen into with her new "dysfunctional" family. She was in better physical shape than half the men hiking up to that cabin, but she was stuck here, twiddling her thumbs. It seemed like she was destined to spend her time as nurse, chief cook, and now babysitter. Not that she wanted to be in some kind of shootout, but she'd like to be seen by Mac as someone capable, smart, and independent. Not someone who needed to be sheltered and protected.

Edgar's cell phone rang breaking the silence.

"Good luck," Edgar said, after listening for a few seconds. "I'll do my best."

He turned to Rachel and nodded. "Mac says they're at the top of the hill. They can see tire tracks but no vehicle. There's a light on in the cabin. They're going in."

Rachel tapped on the window glass and got JJ's attention.

Chapter 15

"Really, now? You can't hold it?"

The Irish wolfhound gave her an incredulous look and Rachel sighed.

Between the snow blocking what little sun there was and the late hour, dusk had settled over their little command center. She wasn't looking forward to wandering around the woods. Whiskey was picky about where she did her business.

"Edgar, I don't suppose–"

"Not me, Ms. Brenner. I have to be ready to drive this van if all hell breaks loose. I can't be out there, walking the dog. Get JJ to do it. She's already frostbitten. Might as well be doing something productive instead of wearing out her boot leather."

Whiskey whined again and nudged Rachel's shoulder.

"Okay. I'll do it. Edgar, hand me those gloves please."

Rachel barely got the door slid open before Whiskey was out it. The good news was that she had a firm grip on the large dog's leash. The bad news was that she had a firm grip on the large dog's leash. Propelled by the dog's forward motion, she managed a face plant when her feet slipped on the icy patch just outside the van. JJ's pacing had melted the snow just enough to create a hazard.

"You all right Ms. Brenner?" Edgar called out to her through the open van door.

Rachel spat out some snow and used an anxious Whiskey's shoulder to lever herself to her feet. "Just fine. Don't trouble yourself."

"Can you close the door then? Losing all the heat in here."

"Sure." Rachel looked around for JJ and spotted her leaning into the window of the trooper's vehicle, having a rather animated discussion.

"Come on girl, let's take care of business and get back inside."

She let the dog wander around, searching for a suitable bush to mark. They were about 50 feet from the van when the sky lit up and the ground shook.

Whiskey lunged, breaking the leash, running the opposite direction from the blast.

JJ screamed and jumped in the trooper's car. He drove off towards the blast, lights and siren's blaring. Rachel couldn't tell if he'd gotten orders over the radio to advance up the hill or if he was just reacting to JJ's demands.

Edgar was shouting at her. She could tell he wanted to follow the trooper's car.

"Don't you go anywhere without me. You won't be able to control JJ anymore than I can. Let the trooper do it." Rachel warned, pointing her finger at the old man. "Have you got a flashlight in there? I have to find Whiskey"

***

Everything had gone according to plan until the first couple of troopers had tried to make entry into the cabin. At the Captain's insistence Mac and the DC detectives were following the West Virginia troopers about twenty feet back. The Arlington County detectives were bringing up the rear.

The concussion from the blast tossed the troopers and Mac's group off their feet and backwards.

"He booby-trapped the door," Fiori yelled. "Be careful, he might have other explosives planted around here."

Mac got to his knees, gun drawn. His ears were ringing and he'd managed to wrench his back again. He looked at the blazing cabin, hoping Randy wasn't inside.

A trooper near the cabin, shouted, "Radio Andrews, tell him to get his car up here. We've got two men down. Have him put out a call for an ambulance!"

"What about a chopper?" Giles asked, giving her partner a hand up. "Think everything is still grounded?"

Mac noticed Jefferson and Mancino circling around the burning structure. Remembering the missing vehicle, he ignored his protesting back muscles and followed. The sound of two gunshots motivated him to move faster.

***

"Where's Randy? Is he dead, Mac?"

JJ was holding on to his coat sleeve, her face paler than he'd ever seen it.

Detective Laura Mancino touched the young woman's arm. "We don't have any reason to believe that. Why don't you go back and wait in one of the cars. You're freezing."

"Mac?" JJ shrugged off the female detective's hand, keeping her eyes on his face. "Is he dead?"

He didn't know what to tell her. There was no sign of the boy. There was only one set of footprints leading from the cabin's back door. They could have been Randy's but more likely they were Doc Alvira's. Detective Jefferson was down near an empty garage where it appeared a car might been parked. There was a back way off the hill. They'd made a mistake. The kidnapper had escaped.

He could see Fiori and Giles poking along the edge of the fire. He knew they were looking for a body, but he didn't tell JJ that. It could be days before they knew for sure what or who might have been in the cabin.

"Mac? Tell me, please." JJ suddenly hugged him, forcing him to put an arm around her just to keep them upright.

Mac coughed; surprised that she would initiate physical contact. Last he knew they weren't exactly speaking. He supposed he'd never understand women.

"My guess is that Doc has him stashed somewhere else." He wasn't exactly lying to her. He just had no idea if her brother was alive. Hope didn't cost anyone anything in this situation. "Where's Rachel and Edgar?"

***

Rachel hesitated for a moment, not sure how to track a dog, who despite her size, could run like a cheetah when spooked.

"Or for a cheeseburger," she muttered to herself.

The tracks took her into a wooded area. The trees offered a respite from the wind and the snow was definitely less deep. But the canopy also blocked the light, so she was surrounded by gloom and darkness.

"Whiskey. Come here girl. Come on; let's get back in the car."

Her voice seemed to get lost in the wind. Rachel marched through snow drifts, calling the dog's name and attempting to whistle like she'd seen Mac do when signaling Whiskey to return.

"There's a reason I have cats. They don't have to go outside to do their business. They're civilized. They believe in indoor plumbing…so to speak." She shook her head, disgusted at her musings and then her need to correct her musings when no one was around to hear them in the first place.

It was too damn cold. She stopped and looked around. The snow was still coming down. No trace of the dog and more alarming, no trace of her footsteps into the woods. Exactly how was she going to find her way out, with or without Whiskey?

"Whiskey? Where are you girl? Bark, Whiskey, Bark."

Rachel listened for a moment, then turned to try and figure out how to get out of the woods when she heard what sounded like a woof.

"Nope, just the wind."

She didn't know how she was going to face Mac without Whiskey. She began to tromp back through the brush, although none of it looked familiar.

"I should have left breadcrumbs, like Hansel and Gretel."

She really had to stop talking to herself, or at least stop speaking out loud. The habit came from too many years of living alone. Even when she was married, it was like living alone, given the lack of communication with her ex-husband.

Plodding through the woods, snow-covered leaves and branches crackling under feet, Rachel might have missed it had she not stopped to decide between two possible paths.

A howl, a strong, Whiskey-howl, came from somewhere to the left of where she was standing.

"I'm coming, Whiskey. I'm coming. Are you stuck girl? Did your leash get hooked on a branch? I'm coming."

She half-ran, slowed by the snow and fallen logs, in the direction of the now constant howling. She stumbled, catching herself before doing another face plant in the snow. She could see Whiskey, pacing and shivering by a large pine tree.

"Okay, girl, I'm here. I'll take you to Mac."

She eased closer to the nervous dog and saw that she was standing guard over someone. Suddenly, Rachel was afraid. Maybe this was Doc and she was about to rescue a killer.

***

The storm was getting worse. Cell phone reception was almost nil. A tower must have been knocked down by the strong winds.

Mac heard the van's horn before he saw the headlights. Edgar was certainly trying to get someone's attention. Mac hoped he hadn't made a terrible mistake in leaving his people alone and unprotected.

"We have to get down this mountain. Alvira is unaccounted for," Mac said, tapping on the driver's side window. He had hiked down the hill and commandeered a squad car to get back to where the van was parked. JJ was still with Fiori and Giles, watching the fire and hoping to find some clue about Randy. Since there was no sign of Doc Alvira's vehicle, Mac had been struck with the sudden fear that the kidnapper had circled round behind the law enforcement group and was a threat to Edgar and Rachel.

Edgar lowered the glass. "Rachel and Whiskey...She had to walk the dog...Didn't come back...Snow...Can't see two feet in front...Might be lost...Hoped she would hear horn." Edgar couldn't get the words out fast enough. "They've been gone too long. Something has happened.

"How long?" Mac asked? He knew neither Rachel nor Whiskey would stay out in the storm longer than absolutely necessary.

"45 minutes. I tried to call you. I couldn't think what to do." Edgar banged his hand against the horn again.

Mac put his hand over the old man's. "Stop. The wind is too strong. They won't be able to hear it. Save the battery for the lights.

As it gets darker, the headlights may be our best hope. I'll take the squad car and drive down the road. If she got turned around, she might have been able to find her way back to the road. You stay here until I come back or some of the others show up."

"Shouldn't I come with you?" Edgar asked. "Where's JJ? What the hell happened? What was that explosion? Did you find the boy?"

"No time to explain everything. We didn't find Randy or Doc Alvira. One of the West Virginia trooper's stepped on a tripwire. Doc Alvira is either naturally paranoid or he intended for us to follow him out here. I don't know what it all means, what his game is, but you stay alert. He might still be around."

"Mac, don't worry about me. I didn't just equip this van with a police radio. My great nephew got me a deal on some personal protection."

"Edgar, you better not be talking about—"

"I'm just saying, don't worry about me. Go on now!"

The snow continued to blow, making it almost impossible for Mac to see the road. He drove slowly, partly because of the vehicle's low clearance and the depth of the snow on the road, but more because there was an excellent chance that even if Rachel and Whiskey were standing right in the middle of the road in front of him, he might not see them.

He would go as far as the convenience store they'd passed about five miles down the road. If he didn't find her, he'd use the store's land line to call for more help.

Rachel and Whiskey were running out of time. Randy's time might have already expired.

Mac tightened his grip on the steering wheel, his eyes moving from one side of the road to the other, praying for a miracle.

***

Rachel started to back away from whoever was on the ground, urging the dog to come with her.

She alternated her stern mother voice, "Whiskey, you come here right now," with her pleading voice, "Please Whiskey, please come here." Neither accomplished anything.

Suddenly, Whiskey ran towards Rachel, who tried to grab her leash. But the dog was too quick and immediately headed back to the figure on the ground, looking over her shoulder to make sure that she was followed.

"Okay, I get the message." Rachel inched forward, holding the flashlight upright like a weapon.

Whiskey curled up next to the figure on the ground, her body a warming blanket of fur.

Rachel knelt down and pushed blond hair off a young, dirty face.

The figure moaned and drew into a tighter ball, knees to chest, eyes shut tight.

Rachel softly stroked an arm. "Randy? Are you Randy? I'm here with your sister. We're looking for you. Mandy is here."

After a moment, the young man's eyes fluttered open. "I want Mandy. He said he would take me to Mandy, but he didn't. I ran away. I'm tired." He then closed his eyes again.

Rachel shook the boy. "Randy, she's here on the mountain. I promise you. Whiskey and I will take you to Mandy. But you've got to get up. You'll freeze to death if we stay here."

She stood up and tried pulling Randy to a standing position, but he was a dead weight. She could hear him repeating softly, "Mandy, Mandy, Mandy."

She couldn't carry him and she couldn't leave him to get help. From his manner, she suspected he'd been drugged.

"Whiskey, stand up."

The dog hesitated a moment, then moved next to her.

She wondered if she could send Whiskey for help, but this wasn't an episode of "Lassie" and it wasn't Timmy down a well.

Rachel pulled and pushed Randy to a seated position.

"Listen to me, Randy. I know you're scared and cold and want to go home, and I'm going to get you there. But you've got to help me. You've got to walk because I can't carry you. Come on Randy, you can do it."

She tugged on his arm and slowly, the young man stood up. He swayed and she caught him as he started to collapse.

"Put your arm around my waist and we'll do this together," she said softly.

Rachel looked around and didn't have a clue how to get out of the woods. But she could smell smoke and decided to follow it hoping it would lead her to the vicinity of the cabin.

Whiskey stood on one side of Randy and Rachel on the other.

"That's right, Randy. We'll go slowly, but we'll get out of here. I promise."

She used the voice that would soothe her own son Sam when he would wake with nightmares.

She glanced at Randy's face. There was a nasty bruise across his cheek, the apparent result of a backhanded smack. His hands were bright red, gloves, if he'd ever had any besides those left at the dentist office, long lost. She took off her own knit gloves and slid them over his fingers, pulled her own knit hat over his head. His pants were torn, but that would have to wait until they got to safety. His sneakers offered little protection in the snow, but that too would have to wait.

The three of them began to walk.

Chapter 16

"Jeff, have you seen these weather reports? This keeps up, we won't be going anywhere tomorrow. Blizzard conditions from DC to Maine and west to Chicago. Any airport that isn't already shut down, is in the process. I hope we don't lose power again. Last time, this happened you promised that we'd buy a generator for the house."

Jeff joined his wife on the sofa, glancing at the excited faces of the weathermen on the 50-inch screen, as he put an arm around her shoulders. "Sorry. I did order one last year, but then it was put on backorder and spring came and...."

She glared at him. "And you got busy taking care of your business and forgot about me and your home."

"I could never forget about you darlin." He grinned. "And what I was about to say was that the generator is in a box in the garage. Perhaps I'll go unpack it and–"

Kathleen shook her head. "And you'll bring me the owner's manual, so we can both read it before you do anything else. I don't want to deal with the after-effects of another fire."

He pulled out his cell phone. "Maybe I'll give Mac a call. I'm going to need some help moving the generator. He owes me a few dozen favors. Time to collect."

"It's late. I'm sure he's asleep by now. Wait until tomorrow." Kathleen switched off the television and got to her feet. "I'm going upstairs to get a hot shower, just in case this is my last chance for a few days. I suggest you do the same."

Jeff glanced at his phone. Despite Kathleen's advice, he felt a sudden urge to call his best friend anyway.

Checking to see that his wife had actually left the room, Jeff keyed in Mac's cell number. His call went right to voice mail.

***

Traveling the five miles down the mountain to the convenience store took almost a half hour. The police cruiser street tires were not designed for driving in thick snow or ice. To get back up the mountain, he was going to need chains or a different ride.

The front doors to the store were locked. The bars on the glass doors were meant to discourage break-ins. They certainly discouraged him.

Mac walked round the small wooden building to the back. He found a small window that was locked but not barred. He used a rock to break the glass and make entry. If the store had a security alarm, it was silent. Truth be told, he'd welcome the arrival of the local police. They'd probably have all-terrain tires on their vehicles.

He tried the phone he found near the cash register. There was a dial tone. He just didn't know who to call first. Out of habit more than any conscious thought, he punched in the number for his best friend, hoping Jeff answered instead of Kathleen.

"Hello?"

"Jeff, it's Mac."

"Of course it is. Who else would it be? Even my kids know not to call this late."

Mac chuckled. He knew Jeff wasn't angry. His old friend was one of the easiest going people he'd ever met. Now Jeff's wife Kathleen, that was another story entirely. Mac figured it was a good ten years into Jeff and Kathleen's marriage before she developed a grudging affection for her husband's best friend. Maybe affection was too strong a term. Amused tolerance might be a more likely description.

"I need some help."

"When have you not?"

"I'm in West Virginia and need a car. Something that can handle deep snow. Oh, and a search-and-rescue team would be nice."

"There's a blizzard going on here in DC"

"Here too. I thought you might know someone who knows someone."

"You're a lucky man to have me for a friend, that's all I can say. I've done business with the Governor's son. Let me find some paper and pen. I'll need some details.

***

The storm was getting stronger. She still felt like a bloodhound, following the scent and occasionally catching sight of the billowing clouds of smoke that were undoubtedly coming from the burning cabin. They were walking uphill in the dark which only added to the struggle. She'd put one gloveless hand in her pocket, but the other one, the hand holding onto Randy's waist, was numb from the cold. She worried about frostbite for both of them, maybe even for Whiskey, although the dog was moving along at a brisk pace beside them.

"Randy, just a little further. We should be coming to the road soon. Then we'll meet Mandy and get in a warm car to go home."

The young man didn't answer. He hadn't said anything for at least fifteen minutes. He was walking, but leaning more and more on her. At first, she'd tried to keep chatting, wanting to reassure him and make sure he was alert, but the driving snow and cold made anything but short conversational bursts impossible.

Suddenly, Randy dropped to his knees, clearly exhausted. "Mandy, where's Mandy?"

She had to remember he'd been out in this weather a lot longer than she had.

Rachel knelt beside him. Whiskey danced over, rubbing her furry face against the almost translucent white cheeks of the young man. The dog whined and nudged, but Randy didn't respond.

Rachel looked around frantically for some shelter from the storm. But there was nothing but trees, snow, and bone-chilling wind. Their best hope, their only hope, was to get to the road. Suddenly, partially covered under a pile of leaves she saw the corner of a vinyl tarp. The type used to cover a cord of stacked wood. They couldn't be that far from a structure.

She quickly brushed off the debris and discovered there were two tarps with pieces of rope threaded through grommets covering the logs. There was even a single worn work glove. A pair would have been nice, but one was better than nothing. She'd gladly wear it.

"Randy, look, we've got a little more protection. I'm going to put this around you and it will help shield the wind. It's not a fur coat, but it's a little help. It will make you look like a Superhero."

She knew she was chattering. She sounded stupid, but she needed to get Randy back on his feet. They had to keep moving or...well...really there was no acceptable alternative.

She tied one tarp around his thin frame and the other around herself.

"Okay Randy, we've got to go now. Think about what you want to eat when we get someplace warm. Hot chocolate with marshmallows or maybe beef stew or a cup of hot tea...."

"Chicken noodle soup. Chocolate chip cookies."

She could barely hear it, but he had mumbled what he wanted to eat. He was still with her, still capable of rational thought, still able to engage in a conversation.

"Let's go then. I think the road is just up ahead. Let's go get you some chicken noodle soup. We'll talk about the cookies afterward. Do you like nuts in your cookies?"

She adjusted the wool hat on his head and they began again.

***

Mac moved the police cruiser to the back of the store. He'd listened to the police scanner long enough to know the state police had abandoned the search for Doc Alvira and were ordering everyone down the mountain for the duration of the storm. He figured that the best way he could help Rachel was to keep a low profile until the cops passed the store, then head back up the mountain to search. He was waiting for a call back from Jeff, hoping he was going to come through for him with a snow plow and a miracle.

***

"I'm not leaving," Edgar told the West Virginia State Police Captain. He was speaking to him through the partially-lowered driver's window. He'd refused to get out of the van or follow the Captain down the mountain. "I've got an extra tank of gas, a good battery, food, water, and patience. Even if Ms. Brenner got turned around in the storm, that dog of Sullivan's is plenty smart. She'll find this van again. I just need to stay put and be here when they come out of those woods."

"Mr. Freed, I'm ordering everyone back to town. County is closing the road." The Captain glared at the old man. "I imagine you're old enough to understand the odds of anyone surviving the night out here. You need to get down off this mountain with the rest of us. You could freeze to death sitting here in this expensive tin can. We'll get a search party out here first thing in the morning."

"No. And I'm old enough to know you can't order me to do anything. It's a free country and I'm of sound mind. Go on with you. I'll be fine. The longer I have to sit here jabbering with you, the more heat leaks out this window."

The van door on the other side slid open and JJ hopped inside, quickly locking it behind her.

"How'd you get that door unlocked?" Edgar asked, abruptly turning his attention from the Captain to his young coworker.

"Extra set of keys," JJ said, dangling them from her hand, before pocketing them. "I had them made in case–"

"No you didn't. You stole them from my house last night!"

"Borrowed." JJ nodded towards the Captain. "Are you really trying to convince him that you're of sound mind?"

"You want to go with them, go on. I'm not moving."

JJ shrugged. "Me neither."

***

It seemed like hours, but it was probably only 30 minutes or so before Randy began to cough from the smoke. It was getting thick. The wind was whipping it around, mixing it with the blowing snow. She couldn't see it yet, but they had to be near the burning cabin.

Rachel pulled up the collar of her coat, trying to block the snow and the fumes. She turned to Randy. "Let me pull your turtleneck over your mouth and nose. Come on, we'll be warm once we get near the fire."

The young man stopped. "No."

She could barely hear him. He refused to take another step.

"Randy, what's wrong. If you look through the trees," she pointed up the incline, "you'll see the flames. It's a cabin. We're almost there."

Randy shook his head. "No. It's his cabin. Won't go there."

Suddenly Rachel understood.

"He's gone. I promise. He died in the explosion. You're safe now, Randy. We just have to get back to the car and your sister. You're safe with me."

The blue eyes looked wary, afraid, and so very young and innocent. A grown man with a child's mind.

Rachel took Randy's hand. "Come on. Let's get some chicken noodle soup."

"Cookies too?"

She nodded. She'd bake him as many cookies as he wanted if they survived the night.

They emerged from the woods on the far side of the burning cabin. The flames were still intense but the heat felt good. Despite what she had told Randy, Rachel wasn't sure at all what had happened to Doc. He might be dead, he might have escaped. But since she didn't hear any bullets whizzing by or bullhorns calling for him to surrender, she figured it was a risk worth taking.

After a few moments of savoring the warmth, she grabbed Randy's hand. "Come on, let's find the others, let's find Mandy."

They circled the area where the cabin had been. Although it was clear the area had been teeming with people only a short time before. It was deserted now. She and Randy were alone.

Whiskey nudged her hand as though to remind her that they weren't entirely alone.

"Where's Mac, girl?

The dog whined.

"I know he won't leave this mountain without you. Me, I'm not so sure about."

Chapter 17

Edgar took a swig of lukewarm coffee from a thermos. "Appears we have some time. Maybe you could explain to me why you lied to Mac about who you really were. I understand all the hiding and running when you were a kid, but I don't see the point after you came of age."

He held the thermos out to her. She shook her head, instead pulling a soda from the cooler on the floor in the passenger area.

"You really that scared of your past?" Edgar asked, pushing for answers from the young woman.

JJ sighed. The old man wasn't going to let go until he got answers. And admittedly he probably deserved some. He was out here, freezing his bony ass off for her and Randy. He sure didn't owe her anything.

"It probably doesn't surprise you to find out that I'm not a nice person," JJ confessed. "I know I'm harsh sometimes–"

"Don't forget prickly. You're prickly," Edgar interjected. "Prickly and stubborn."

JJ took a deep breath, visibly trying to hold on to her temper. "Fine. But I don't need your help telling my life story, old man. You wanted to hear this, now shut up and listen."

"Disrespectful, too."

She took a drink of her soda. "Anything else?"

"Ungrateful. You wear ugly clothes. And you cut your hair too short."

She could see him watching her in his rear view mirror.

"Is that it?" Her expression had darkened as she'd listened to his list of complaints.

He finished his coffee. "Loyal, brave, smart as a whip, and someone I'd want to share a foxhole with."

Confused, she clamored over the console into the front passenger seat. "Foxhole? Why the hell would–"

"Never mind. Go on with your story minus the profanity. I'm getting older by the minute. If you don't hurry up, I'll be senile by the time you finish."

"You're–"

He smiled at her.

Cagey. He was cagey. She swallowed the comeback she'd almost dished out. Nothing wrong with his mind. The old man was smarter than most people gave him credit for, she'd give him that.

"You're wrong about my clothes." She glanced down at her ripped jeans. She'd put the rips in herself about two years ago. Might have over done it. "Mostly."

Edgar reached out his hand and patted her shoulder. "Tell me about Amanda."

***

The storm got worse and Rachel gave up her plan to walk down the road. The snow was blowing too hard to try to stumble down the road towards the nearest town. At the moment they weren't lost. Rachel wanted to keep it that way. They set up camp in the garage, waiting for daybreak.

Garage was probably the wrong term. It was more like a large shed or small barn, she wasn't sure a car would have ever fit inside, even if one had been parked in front. The structure wasn't insulated, had no floor and was open on one end. But it gave them a roof over their heads and proximity to the warmth from the fire. She used a board to clear the snow that had blown inside, creating a place for the tarps she and Randy had been wearing.

"You said there would soup," Randy reminded her as they sat down. "Isn't it past dinner time?"

"Way past," she agreed. "I'm hungry too."

Whiskey whined, pacing back and forth under the shelter. The wolfhound was obviously distressed that they weren't moving.

"I know girl. But I'm not sure I can find my way down the mountain. With the darkness and the snow, I'd be walking blind."

"Whiskey, come." Randy called to the dog. "I need to brush the snow off you."

Rachel was grateful the dog took the boy's mind off his own situation even for a little while. Getting to her feet, she walked over to study the locked closet at the far end of the building. The combination lock looked too strong to break, but the hasp holding it was only screwed into one of the wooden doors. With some effort she might be able to remove the hasp and open the closet. She doubted there was chicken noodle soup or cookies inside, but she might find something of use. Their survival might depend on it.

***

"The last time Amanda Norman was truly happy was when she was eight-years-old and was picked to be a sugar plum fairy in a grade school play. She only stayed happy long enough to get home and share the news with her drunken mother who could not have cared less about her daughter's small social success. Amanda was told that they had no money for foolishness, assuming that a costume would be involved and she'd be expected to provide it. The next day, a tearful Amanda told her teacher her mother said 'no' to the play and her daughter's starring role."

Edgar listened without interruption, wondering at JJ's third person account of the child she used to be. Perhaps it was how she really saw herself–two people; the person she was before she ran away and the one afterward.

"Randy was almost three before Amanda realized there was something wrong with him. Something more than a clean diaper and a full bottle would cure. He'd sit on the floor and scream for no reason. Amanda's mother would leave when the noise got to her. At six, Amanda had nowhere to go. She carried him around a lot, he seemed to like being held."

She paused and Edgar asked, "Where was your...Amanda's father during all this?"

JJ sighed. "Good question. I don't have an answer. He died when Amanda was ten, but before that? No clue. Amanda saw him a half dozen times in her entire life. He drove a truck when he was sober. He was unemployed more often than not."

"Your...Amanda's mother is dead?" Edgar had read that much in one of the files Mac had given him about the Amanda Norman disappearance.

"Killed herself the year Amanda started third grade. Overdosed on pills and booze. Social Services took control. There were a series of foster homes. Randy didn't do well with change and there was lots of change. Amanda and Randy eventually landed with Uncle Hugo and Lisa, his wife. Randy liked Lisa. They stayed three years. Then Randy...he...he got worse."

"Worse?"

JJ sighed. "He became violent. He doesn't mean to hurt anyone, but he has trouble controlling his anger. After he was put in the special school, he was on meds to even out his moods. The drugs work. I don't think he's had an incident in years. But back then, when he was living with Uncle Hugo, there was an incident with a knife."

Edgar didn't like the direction this conversation was going. No one had mentioned anything to him about Randy needing to be on medication. Nothing about him being dangerous. "Randy used a knife to...what?"

JJ took a deep breath. "Randy cut off the tip of Uncle Hugo's finger when he tried to take away something that Randy was playing with. Some figurine from one of Uncle Hugo's heists. There was always junk laying around. But Randy fixated on a certain thing and Uncle Hugo didn't want him touching it. I think Uncle Hugo would have killed Randy that day but for Lisa's intervention. But it was the beginning of the end for Amanda and Randy's life there."

Edgar tried to figure out how long the kid would have been without his medication. Best case scenario? Too long.

Chapter 18

"Mac Sullivan." Mac held out his hand to the very large man who'd just arrived at the convenience store driving a snow plow.

"Carson Douglas, we seem to have mutual friends, Mr. Sullivan."

Mac winced as the man's beefy hand grasped his in a steel grip. "Call me, Mac. I've very glad to see you. I need to get up this mountain tonight. Can you help me?"

"Won't be easy, Mac. But then if it was easy, you wouldn't have needed to pull strings all the way from DC to Charleston. I'm being well-compensated to risk my neck and equipment getting you up this road, but are you sure you want to go now? Much safer to travel in daylight when the odds are better that we'll stay on the road. You know there's no shoulder on the left side, just a 300-foot drop to the bottom? We go down that way, we won't be coming back up."

Mac nodded. "I'm sure. Let's go."

***

"What did...Amanda do when she and Randy were separated?"

Edgar looked at his watch. It had been more than three hours since the cabin exploded and Rachel chased after Whiskey into a blinding snowstorm. He shifted in his seat. He kept turning the engine on and off, trying to keep some heat in the van, but also keep enough gasoline for them to get off the mountain once the storm let up. The cold wasn't good for his emphysema, arthritis, or nerves.

He realized that JJ hadn't answered him. She was at the edge of the seat, staring out the window, probably trying to figure out her next move.

He touched her shoulder and she flinched. He withdrew his fingers.

"You got to be here when they find your brother. If you're lost in the storm on some fool rescue mission, no telling what the boy will do. Just settle back. Mac ain't let us down yet; he's not about to start now."

JJ began to object, but stopped. After a moment she scooted back into her seat, but continued to scan the scene outside the van.

Edgar turned on the engine once more, the heat blowers flooding them with warmth. He'd give it two minutes, maybe three.

"Amanda was never the same once they separated her from Randy. She knew they were wrong about Randy needing a special school and special treatment. She knew how to take care of him. Always had, always would."

The young woman's voice was getting shakier. Edgar could hear tremors as she spoke; thought he even glimpsed JJ roughly brushing something from her cheek.

Edgar reluctantly turned off the engine and tightened his coat.

He could barely hear her, her voice scarcely a whisper. "I'm going to take Randy to some place warm when this is all over. I've got the money, you know. Think he'd like Disney World? Or maybe

Sea World. Randy's always liked animals. That's why I took Whiskey to the group home. I knew that Randy would love to play with her. He's real gentle with animals."

Edgar leaned his head back against the window. "We took our girl to Disney World when it first opened. Spent the money and stayed right in the park. My wife thought it cost too much, called it 'foolishness,' but I was always glad we'd done it. I still can remember my girl's face when she met Cinderella. Never seen anybody that happy before or since. We went on every ride in the place. Wife sat them out, but not me. Even went on that Space Mountain. As we were going up to the top, my girl said, 'You won't let go of me, will you Daddy?' And I didn't, not for one second. Held onto her tight as tick on a fat country dog. Strange to think she'd be a little older than Ms. Brenner now if she was alive."

The two sat is silence, both lost in warm memories on a frigid night.

Suddenly, JJ opened her door.

Edgar was shocked out of his visit to happier times by the blast of cold air and snow. "What in tarnation are you doing? I thought we agreed that we'd stay put until Mac got here. Close the door before we freeze to death."

JJ shook her head. "I heard something."

"Just the wind and wishing. Close the door and I'll turn on the heat."

JJ stepped out of the van. "No, old man, I heard a motor, like a snowmobile or maybe…"

Then, he heard it too. Out of the darkness he saw powerful headlights. Something was heading straight for the darkened van, the one no one could see through the drifting snow.

"Get in, you fool. I've got to move before they run us down."

Edgar turned the key. The engine sputtered, once, twice, but finally caught. He turned the headlights on.

JJ jumped back in and slammed the door as he put the van in gear and leaned on the horn. If whoever was coming couldn't see them, maybe he'd hear them.

***

Rachel glanced back at Randy sitting with Whiskey just inside the garage. For the moment he seemed content to brush the snow from the big dog's fur while humming a nameless tune slightly off-key.

Using a long stick, she continued searching the smoldering edges of the cabin's remains, looking for a piece of metal that she might use to pry the hasp from the doors of the garage's locked closet. After a half hour of battling the blowing snow, she'd only managed to salvage three tin cans, a cracked ceramic lamp minus its shade, a canvas shopping bag, and a metal bucket that had probably once held kindling for the fireplace.

She scooped up some still glowing ashes from the fire into the bucket and carried it and the canvas bag full of her other finds back to the garage. "Randy, I found some canned food but the labels have burned off. Might be something good if we can find a way to get the cans open. We could set the cans in this bucket and have something hot to eat."

He looked at her and the cans. "Might be green beans. I don't like green beans. Or peas. What if it's peas?"

"I doubt all three are beans or peas. We might get lucky."

His expression led her to conclude he thought the chances of that were pretty slim.

She sighed. Randy was right. Apparently neither of them were lucky people.

Randy reached out and pulled the lamp out of the bag. He studied the metal light socket. Without warning he slammed the lamp against the ground, startling both Whiskey and Rachel.

Clearing away the pottery, he twisted the metal tubing until he had a straight length of pipe. He looked at the locked closet and then handed the pipe to her.

Rachel smiled. "I'll give it a try. Maybe there will be a knife or can opener in there."

He nodded and resumed his seat. Stroking the dog, he muttered, "No peas."

Chapter 19

The snow plow was climbing up the mountain road faster than Mac had expected. The plan was to clear a lane while they went, so hopefully Edgar's van could make it down afterwards. Carson Douglas, the tow driver, had thought to bring a set of chains for the van. He was also carrying extra gas and a handheld GPS unit.

It was just past four a.m. and the temperatures were in the low twenties. The wind was whipping the snow, making visibility a constant issue.

"About six or seven more miles to the top," Carson said. "Then we'll be near the cabin location. How far away did you say your van was parked from the top of the ridge?"

"Maybe two miles, a little less." Mac was worried about a dozen different things, but Carson's driving ability wasn't one of them. The man seemed to know his business and how to maneuver in bad weather. Dawn was a couple of hours away. He hoped Edgar, JJ, and Rachel were holding on; hoped they knew he would do everything he could to get them home. Ironically the only one he wasn't worried too much about was Whiskey. She'd eventually come back to the van if she was able.

"Going to be tricky seeing the vehicle ahead of time." Carson tapped the GPS unit he'd hung from the dash. "Keep an eye on that. I plugged in the approximate coordinates for the cabin before we left.

215

When we get close, I'll slow down and with a little luck, we'll see your people before we're right on top of them."

***

Rachel shimmied the pipe between the closet door and the frame. She pushed and pulled, hoping to loosen the hinge that was surprisingly strong. Finally, after a final jiggle, the closet door swung open.

"Alright. We're in business."

Randy and Whiskey looked up briefly, but quickly returned to adoring and being adored. The dog might be cold, but knew a devoted fan when she was near one.

But business didn't mean food. Instead, Rachel found a gun cabinet built inside. There was a lone handgun wrapped in an oil cloth and boxes of bullets on one shelf along with several knives. There were two empty shelves below that, dust patterns indicating they had recently been filled with something, probably weapons. There were empty spaces to the side where rifles or shotguns would have been stored. Boxes of shells were stacked on the floor. Doc Alvira was a survivalist. If he got out of the cabin alive, he was well-armed.

Rachel gripped the side of the closet, barely able to stand. If the fire had gotten any closer, if the wind had shifted, the bullets would have exploded. Randy, Whiskey, and she would have....

216

She shook her head. She didn't have time for the coulda happened. It hadn't. Maybe they were luckier than Randy thought, even if all the cans were peas and green beans.

Grabbing the handgun, she was surprised at its weight. She'd need both hands to fire it, but if Doc Alvira was still anywhere in the area, she and Randy might need the protection.

She again shook off those thoughts. She checked to see if it was loaded, slipped the gun into her pocket, threw in a box of bullets, and snatched a large hunting knife from the shelf. She pasted a smile on her face for Randy's benefit. She turned around.

"Okay. No can opener, but I bet we can pierce the tops with this." She brandished the knife. Randy's eyes got big as saucers.

It took several attempts, but she finally managed to open the cans. The first two contained beef stew. The third one was indeed the dreaded green peas. A few minutes in the smoldering embers and dinner was served. She gave most of the stew to Randy and Whiskey, both of whom declined the green vegetable.

The trio ate in silence. When they'd finished, Rachel threw the empty tins into a trash can. She smiled at her need to clean up even in a garage in the middle of a blizzard.

"Where's Mandy? You said she'd be here."

His tone was like a little boy who'd been promised a bike for Christmas and ended up with socks.

Rachel sat down beside Randy. "She couldn't get up the mountain in the storm. She's waiting for you at the bottom. We'll head down there at daybreak. By then, the snow will have ended."

"Promise?"

Rachel nodded.

Randy leaned back against the garage wall and within moments was fast asleep. Whiskey followed suit. She curled up close to the young man, snoring softly, her head in his lap.

Rachel shifted in place, trying to stay warm and awake. She took the gun out of her pocket and placed it next to her leg. If anyone but Mac Sullivan came through the door of the garage, she'd be ready.

***

"I need to clear the snow off the van's lights, they can't see us," JJ said, opening the door again.

"Keep your skinny butt in that seat, Missy. I can't stop. No traction." Edgar had the van moving but it wasn't headed in any particular direction.

"Edgar, turn to the right. We're going to slide off the road if you're not careful."

"No screaming. Screaming gets on my nerves. I know what I'm doing."

"Well, I'm warning you right now, riding this van to the bottom of a ravine will inspire a lot of screaming on my part, old man."

"Okay, that looks like a turnaround. Should be enough room for a truck or whatever that is behind us to pass."

"You don't know what's under that snow."

"No, I don't but I don't plan to be a hood ornament on whatever's coming up behind us. Sometimes you just have to take the least bad option and commit to it."

"Yeah." JJ sighed. "I know all about bad options."

***

Rachel awoke with a start. "Damn. You weren't supposed to sleep. Some bodyguard you are." She whispered to herself, trying to shake the cobwebs loose from her brain. Her heart was beating so loud and fast that she was sure she'd waken Randy and Whiskey. But neither moved a muscle. The dog snored softly.

What was it? She strained to hear. Maybe distant thunder. She picked up the gun and crawled slowly to the garage's open doorway. A quick peek outside confirmed that the snow had stopped. The cabin was now just fiery embers, and the dawn was peeking through the dark sky. She couldn't see anyone, but the muffled rumbling continued.

She stood, even holding the gun in both hands, it felt heavy, like a 20-pound dumbbell in the gym. Surely, it didn't weigh that much. She held it out in front of her, like she'd seen in countless television procedurals, and ducked outside, flattening herself against the wall.

"Like Charlie's Angels," she whispered, and assumed a crouch position, arms outstretched, gun pointing straight ahead, and pivoted 180-degrees to survey the surrounding area. "Okay, that felt stupid."

Nothing, except the constant rumbling, now getting louder. Was it help? Or a killer on a snowmobile coming back to his cabin? Go back in the garage and wait, or confront whoever, take him out before he took them out? Shoot for the head? Shoot for the chest? Shoot the snowmobile and maybe he'd be thrown and she wouldn't have to figure out if she was capable of killing someone?

She barely had seconds to consider. Whatever was making the noise was just over the ridge. She spotted the beams from large headlights before she saw the vehicle. She assumed the stance again.

It was a huge snowplow, but she couldn't see the driver and passenger.

Whiskey came charging out of the garage and ran full tilt towards the plow.

"Whiskey, stop, stop." She put the gun in her pocket and ran after the hairy hound. "Damn it dog, this is how we got into trouble in the first place."

The plow ground to a halt and Whiskey stood at the passenger's side, barking furiously. Rachel caught up just as the door opened and Whiskey began leaping into the air, all four feet off the ground.

"Thank God, you're okay," came a familiar welcome voice.

Rachel grinned. "You'd better be talking about both of us."

Mac dropped to the ground and swept her up in a tight embrace. She could barely breathe and didn't mind for a second. Then he kissed her until she had no breath left at all.

Whiskey danced around the couple, excited and happy.

"I found Randy." She mumbled when he finally stooped to quiet Whiskey.

"What?" Mac stood up quickly. "Is he okay? Where is he?"

She pointed back to the garage. "Fast asleep in there, or he was. He might be awake and too scared to come out."

Mac started towards the garage, with Rachel and Whiskey close behind. Suddenly, Whiskey dashed into the structure, just ahead of Mac.

"Get off me. Get off me."

Mac and Rachel reached the doorway to find Whiskey on Randy's chest, gripping the young man's right arm in her mouth. Randy was struggling to push the dog off him, while scrambling with his left hand to find the hunting knife that was just out of reach.

Mac kicked the knife out of the way, then pulled on Whiskey's collar to get her off the boy. "He probably needs his medication. Edgar and the van are right behind us."

Rachel reached out to help Randy up. "It's okay, it's okay. Mac's a friend of your sister's. He's here to take you to her."

Randy was still agitated, fighting to break loose of Rachel's grip.

"You're lying. You don't know Mandy. You said she'd be here. You said—"

"Randy."

It was like slow-motion in the movies. Randy went limp and slid to the ground. JJ, aka Mandy, rushed to his side.

"I'm here, Randy. I'm always going to be here for you. Shh, shh."

The street-tough assistant was suddenly transformed into a mother, cradling her not-so-little brother and whispering words of comfort. Randy clung to her like a lifeline.

The quiet sweetness of the brother-sister reunion was shattered by a familiar voice.

"Mac we've got a problem." Edgar stood in the doorway of the garage. The plow driver stood next to him. And Rachel could see a gun pointed at both of them.

Edgar continued. "I'd like you to meet Doc Alvira."

Chapter 20

"Good to see you Amanda. Your little brother is the same pain in the ass he always was, but you...you've grown up into quite the woman."

Rachel had never seen such a sinister smile. If blood could curdle, she was sure hers just had. She moved closer to the brother and sister huddled together. So had Mac.

"Sorry, I can't be quite the hospitable host. My house is...." Alvira waved around his rifle, "Quite a mess. You'll have to stop by another time when I can entertain you properly...or not."

He poked the gun into Edgar's back, pushing him into the garage. The old man stumbled, but the snow plow driver caught his arm.

"So, what have we got here. An ex-cop," Alvira pointed the weapon at Mac. "Yes indeed, I know who you are Mr. Mackenzie Sullivan. Fancy yourself as quite the private detective, do you? Think you're like one of those private eyes on TV, but you didn't even know that I was watching you from one floor above that two-bit office you've got."

Alvira laughed, then pointed the weapon at Randy, who buried his head in JJ's shoulder. "And then we've got this whiny, sniveling pissant who literally didn't have the good sense to get out of the rain or should I say snow. But not to worry, looks like his big sister was there to save his sorry ass. She was always such a pain about how nobody should hurt poor stupid little Randy."

JJ started to stand, but Mac put a hand on her shoulder to keep her in place.

Mac confronted the gunman. "Okay, Alvira. What do you want? If you get out of here right now, you might have an hour's lead before the cops are swarming this mountain looking for you. Leave us here and we'll muddle through until help comes."

Alvira laughed again. Rachel thought he sounded like a bad imitation of Jack Nicholson as the Joker.

She put her hand in her jacket pocket. The gun she'd taken from the garage was there. She was well aware that having it might get her or someone else killed. For the moment she'd leave it where it was.

Alvira laughed again. "You're almost as stupid as that kid, Sullivan. You really think I'm leaving here without the coins? I've invested too much time to leave them behind. Now listen up, Miss Amanda or do you prefer being called JJ?"

The young woman shook off Mac's hand and got to her feet. "I don't know what you are ranting about. What do you want? Leave Randy out of this and you can have my money and anything else I've got. Just leave my brother alone, you miserable bastard."

"Bitch." Alvira spat out the word. "You think you've got enough money in the bank to make all this worthwhile? Your money couldn't get me out of this one-horse town, let alone to someplace permanently warm. You know exactly what I want. I want the coins from that shipwreck, the ones Hugo stole from that exhibit. We did that job together and he skipped with my share. Where are the damn coins? Idiot Randy didn't know what I was talking about...but you do, don't you? Hugo swore you must have taken them when Social Services yanked you out of his house. He tried to find you when he got out of prison. But like everything else in his life, he failed miserably. Sending those damn postcards to Sullivan all those years, what the hell did he think that was going to accomplish?"

Edgar cleared his throat.

Alvira laughed again. "Okay, I'll give him that one. The great detective Mac Sullivan finally managed to find Amanda after she parked herself in his office." He waved the gun in JJ's direction. "And now you're going to give them to me or watch your brother and all your friends here die. Maybe to get things started right I'll shoot off one of your brother's fingers just to even the score for Hugo."

Mac stepped in front of JJ and Randy, while Rachel moved closer.

Rachel considered how she might get the gun to Mac but decided it was too risky. Alvira seemed to be a lot of talk at the moment.

"You going to be a hero, Mr. Sullivan? I think not." He pointed the gun at Rachel. "Not if you don't want your girlfriend's pretty body riddled with bullets. I've been watching you two for the last month. Touching. The ex-cop finds true happiness at last. Too bad it's going to be short-lived if your little assistant doesn't step up and give me those coins."

JJ pushed past Mac. "Let's go. Leave these losers here. I'll go with you and get the coins. We have to go back to DC, but we don't need any extra baggage."

Alvira stared at the young woman, then shook his head. "No, we're going to do this my way. You've got 15 hours Amanda Norman to figure out how to get down this mountain and get me the coins. I'll meet you in front of the Air and Space Museum at midnight. Sort of a sentimental choice, don't you think? It's where Amanda Norman died, so to speak, and the quest for my fortune began.

He nudged Rachel with his gun. "By the way, I'm taking cupcake here as insurance that none of you invite the cops to our party. We'll just keep this private, shall we?"

"Take me with you instead," Mac offered. "Rachel's going to be a drag on you. I'll go and the rest of them can get back on their own. I can negotiate with any cops who are on your trail."

Alvira snorted. "You're pathetic. Some Knight in Shining Armor you make. No, I think I'll stick to my plan. Of course, I'll need your gun before I leave. Just to make sure that it's an even playing field, so to speak. You cops are always so trigger happy and I think you were considered quite the marksman in your day."

Mac slowly handed him his gun. "She gets so much as a paper cut and you'll die a slow, lingering, very painful death. It's a promise."

Alvira laughed. He roughly grabbed Rachel's shoulder and jerked her next to him. He kept her with him as they began backing out of the garage.

With his gun in one hand, Alvira used the other to grab the keys to the snow plow. He tossed them into the ashes of the cabin. Then he shot one of the tires on Edgar's van. "That should give us a good head start. I'll see you at midnight Sullivan. Don't be late."

Rachel didn't offer any resistance as he led her off into the woods.

***

Carson Douglas, the snow plow driver, had a spare set of keys and a better jack than Edgar had in his van. He had Edgar's tire changed in record time.

Mac was impressed. The man was prepared for just about everything. Well, everything except a crazed killer with a gun. Carson agreed to keep quiet about the incident, but Mac had a feeling Jeff had just used up more favors than he'd intended.

They followed Carson down the winding mountain road. The snow had stopped but the road was icy and treacherous. Mac offered to drive but Edgar insisted on keeping control of his van. Truthfully, Mac was grateful for the time it allowed him to consider his options. He was going to have to contact the police but as in most things, timing was everything.

***

Rachel was beyond tired. She was cold, hungry, and worried about the gun in her pocket. Doc Alvira hadn't searched her, but he kept her in front of him. They walked through knee-deep snow to get to the SUV that Alvira had stashed on a forestry road about a half mile from the cabin.

"You drive," he demanded, handing her the keys.

"I'm not sure...." She took a good look at his expression and shut up. If she landed them in a ditch, so be it. It was going to be a long trip.

The trip down the mountain was treacherous, but the four-wheel drive provided some traction on the slippery slope. Rachel concentrated so hard on maneuvering the monster of a vehicle that she almost forgot that she had a lunatic with a gun in the seat next to her. When they finally emerged on the highway, she hadn't a clue where they were or where they were going.

"Left here, then right on Jackson Drive about a half mile up."

Rachel followed his directions, but Jackson Drive, was basically an unpaved road that seemed to cut through a forest.

"Where are we going?" The SUV bounced along, hitting the bottom of craters hidden by snow and bouncing back up, jarring her back, already sore from the earlier trek with Randy.

Alvira was checking something on his phone. "Just drive."

Rachel sighed. "Look, at some point, I've got to use the bathroom. Are we going anywhere near civilization or..."

Alvira ignored her, skimming something he'd found on his phone.

After about another mile, Jackson Drive ended at what appeared to be a state road. At least a plow had been through in the last hour, judging from the piles of snow on the sides of the road and the layer of salt covering the asphalt.

She stopped the car. "Now what?"

Alvira was still engrossed in whatever was on his phone. He finally looked up. "Take a right. We'll be on Route 25 for a couple of hours."

Rachel wondered what would happen if she just jumped out of the SUV and made a run for it. Would he shoot her before her feet touched the ground? He certainly didn't care about killing anyone in his way. But he needed her. Mac would undoubtedly demand to see her before turning over whatever the hell Alvira wanted. She fingered the gun in her pocket. Who was she kidding? It was one thing to play Charlie's Angels, it was another to actually know how to shoot the damn thing and kill him. Because one thing was sure, if he wasn't dead, Alvira would kill her for trying.

"I said take a right." Alvira gestured with his gun.

"Where are we going?"

Alvira hesitated for a moment, then shrugged. "Arlington. We'll wait out your boyfriend and those brats. See if they really care if you live or die. Now move it."

***

"Why are you wearing sunglasses inside? You aren't supposed to wear sunglasses inside buildings. You won't be able to see."

A much calmer Randy asked Mac the question while waiting for another plate of pancakes to be delivered to the table.

They were about three hours from DC. Except for two brief stops at convenience stores to get gas and snacks, they hadn't stopped. Finally Edgar had demanded they take an hour and get some hot food and as he called it, "fully-leaded coffee."

Mac had to admit, the stop was a good idea. They were all hungry and exhausted. He took another sip of coffee and managed a smile for the young man. "I don't need to see. I have Whiskey to lead me around. She likes to pretend she's a service dog. I'm humoring her."

Randy looked at the Irish wolfhound sitting next to Mac's chair. The dog had finished off an equal number of pancakes, although she'd declined the syrup. Like Randy, she was waiting for a second round.

JJ sighed, pushing scrambled eggs around on her plate. "This is all my fault. I've dragged all of you into my trouble, almost got Randy killed, and now Rachel is in danger. I don't know how to fix this."

"I agree. It is your fault," Edgar said, holding up his empty cup and waving the waitress over. "You need to learn to trust people and stop thinking you have to fix everything on your own. Take me for instance. I'm trusting Mac to have a plan to handle this."

Mac was glad of the dark glasses. At Edgar's words all eyes at the table trained on him for a response. A plan? Yeah, right. As if that was something he could just pick off a menu and have delivered along with his fried eggs. He was worried about Rachel. He believed Doc Alvira would keep her safe until he got what he wanted from JJ, but what about afterward? Any ransom handoff was tricky. He'd have to bring the police in, but when? And who? There were too many jurisdictions involved now: West Virginia, Virginia, Washington DC...and the Feds. FBI probably had a dog in the fight now. He was going to have to be very careful or he'd become trapped in the red tape that was forming around this case.

Case? Who was he kidding. It wasn't just a case. It was more than that. It was family. JJ, her brother, Edgar, Whiskey, and now Rachel—they were all depending on him.

"Everybody hurry up and finish. We've got to get back on the road. No more stops until we get to DC."

Chapter 21

"Randy, do you remember when we lived with Uncle Hugo?"

JJ, Randy, and Edgar were sitting in Edgar's living room. Having showered and changed, they were waiting for Mac and Whiskey to return. The television was airing a basketball game that had been holding Randy's attention for the last hour.

"Yes. I had my own room but I was too scared to sleep there by myself. So he gave me Roger. I have my own room at the group home. It's nicer. But I don't have Roger. Do you know where Roger is?"

"Who's Roger?" Edgar asked, booting up his laptop computer. "I don't remember a Roger in all this mess."

"Roger was a parakeet," JJ answered. "He went to bird heaven a long time ago."

"Bird heaven. That means he's dead," Randy said for Edgar benefit. "JJ doesn't like to say the word 'dead'."

JJ smiled. "Randy, do you remember the special coins that Uncle Hugo kept in his bedroom?"

"Pirate coins. We weren't supposed to touch them." Randy shook his head. "Uncle Hugo told me they were cursed. What's cursed?"

"Never mind. Uncle Hugo was joking. He really liked those coins but he lost them. His brother wants them. Do you know where they might be?"

"Where is Uncle Hugo? Is he still mad at me about the knife?"

"No. He's not angry with anyone anymore. He's gone to be with Roger. Do you know where those coins went?"

"Aunt Lisa was sick. Is she dead too?"

Edgar frowned. "Lisa? That was Hugo's wife?"

JJ nodded. "She didn't survive long enough to have a kidney transplant and that's why I was moved to another foster home. Plus Hugo got arrested. Randy was already in Bainbridge by then."

"Bainbridge? The state school that—"

"Yeah." JJ shook her head. "It was a dump. It burned down not long after Randy was put there. They sent all the students back into foster homes and group homes. That's why I had problems tracking him."

"Aunt Lisa made me brownies." Randy turned to Edgar. "Do you have brownies?"

Edgar laughed. "No, but I can get some. I have several lady friends who'd like nothing better than to bake up a bunch of brownies for me. I'll put out the word, I've got a craving. First, though you answer your sister's question about the coins. What happened to them?"

Randy shrugged. "Aunt Lisa hid them. I promised not to tell."

"Do you like those brownies with chocolate icing on top?" Edgar asked, pulling out his cell phone. "We could pick some up on our way to find the coins, if we knew where to look."

"I know what you're doing. I'm not stupid," Randy said. "You're bribing me. Brownies for the pirate coins."

Edgar nodded. "Yes, I am."

JJ smiled at her brother. "What do you think? Aunt Lisa won't care anymore. That was a long time ago."

"I like chocolate icing on top, but no nuts," Randy warned. "No nuts."

***

"Thanks for the help with the snow plow," Mac said. He, Jeff, and Whiskey were in the Sullivan Investigations office. "And for the use of your car."

"You're welcome for the snow plow, but not so fast about my Mercedes. I'm coming with it."

"So am I." Kathleen O'Herlihy emerged from the office bathroom.

"Jeff, Kathleen, thanks, but no thanks. I've got way too many players at the table as it is." Mac continued rummaging through files on the conference table until he came up with a small notebook; the notebook he'd used during the original Amanda Norman investigation..

"Yes, but if things go south, you really going to rely on Edgar and JJ to cover your back? You know I'm licensed to carry. Greeley helped me get it."

"What gun?"

Mac watched as the old-married couple had a conversation without any words. Jeff shrugged, Kathleen shook her head, and it was clear that the discussion would be continued.

Mac nodded. "After the stuff with the funeral home takeover attempts, I remember you said you were going to get one."

"I did." Jeff turned from Kathleen to face his friend. "Anyway, what's the plan?"

"Why does everyone assume I can whip up a plan out of thin air?" Mac grumbled. He walked into his office and moved a full-length overcoat off a hook on the wall. The coat had covered the door to a small safe. He punched in a code and the door unlocked. He pulled out an envelope with his emergency cash and a backup handgun.

"Did you call Greeley?"

Mac sighed. "Yeah, about a half hour ago. He's pissed. He still had detectives up on that mountain looking for me...and the kid. I think I might have used up all my chips with him for the next five years."

"What about Rachel?"

"He's going to hold off on the APB and give me a chance to set up the exchange with Doc Alvira. I'm going to have Fiori and Giles stuck to me like glue once they get back from West Virginia so I've got to move fast."

Jeff nodded. "Well until Fiori and Giles catch up with you, you'll have to put up with me."

"Us," Kathleen said firmly. "I'll drive and keep the car running, while you and Jeff do what you need to do. What's next?"

Mac stared at his old friends, knowing he wasn't going to be able to talk them out of it. Truth was, he really did need their help, but he hated involving them in yet another dangerous situation. "Fine. I don't have time to argue with you."

"And not to put too fine a point on it, I have the car," Jeff added.

Kathleen held up her hand. "And I have the keys."

Jeff looked at his wife, then laughed. "Right."

Mac put his coat back on and started turning out lights.

Jeff, Kathleen, and Whiskey followed him into the outer office. "So I repeat...what's next?"

Mac shook his head. "A treasure hunt for pirate gold."

***

Mac motioned for Edgar to lower the driver's window. "How's he doing?"

Edgar shrugged, putting the van in park and motioning towards JJ to answer.

JJ's smile was tight and brief. "Better. I managed to get Randy his meds, but he's still anxious. He's...." She didn't want to tell Mac more than she had to about her brother's wild mood swings and past incidents of violent behavior. It didn't matter anyway. Randy was the only one living who might know where Uncle Hugo's gold coins were hidden. And they needed those coins to save Rachel. "He'll be okay."

The house was small and dingy. They went in through the backyard. The snow was melting in patches, exposing the lack of grass. There was a rusted basketball hoop, nailed to a big oak. The tree's roots had cracked the ten-by-ten-foot concrete slab mercilessly, making it impossible now to actually play a game on the surface.

JJ stopped and stared. "It wasn't this bad when we lived here. Course there were cracks even then. I always had bruised knees and skinned elbows. Living with Uncle Hugo was always like that— danger always lurking just under the surface, ready to trip you up."

"JJ?" Mac held the backdoor open.

He could see her shake her head, clearing the memories that clung to her skin along with moisture dripping from the tree branches. The weather reports had indicated this was a brief lull before the next storm front arrived. They were fighting time in more ways than one.

"Is Uncle Hugo here?" Randy asked, hesitating before following JJ through the doorway. "Are you sure he's not still mad at me? Did they sew his finger back on?"

Edgar put a hand on the young man's shoulder. "Don't you worry about Uncle Hugo. He can't bother you anymore."

JJ held out her hand to her brother. "Remember, he's dead. Aunt Lisa is dead. No one is here but my friends."

Randy seemed unconvinced until Whiskey nudged him, wanting to go inside out of the cold. He smiled. "Okay. Can I see my old room? Is Roger there?"

"Roger's dead, too." JJ called back over her shoulder as she walked through the kitchen. Most of the furnishings were gone, the linoleum faded and torn.

"But maybe his cage is still here?" Randy persisted. "Aunt Lisa painted it yellow. Remember Roger really liked it."

"Sure, it might still be here." She turned and smiled at him. "We'll check upstairs."

Edgar shuffled in, his portable oxygen tank strapped to his back. "I'm not going up any stairs. I'll look around down here. I wonder if Hugo always thought JJ took the coins? If so, he might not have looked too hard for them here. His wife could have hid them in plain sight."

Jeff, exchanging glances with Mac, indicated he'd stay downstairs with Edgar.

Mac knew his friend was staying behind to make sure they weren't surprised by Doc Alvira or someone he might have hired to keep watch on them. Kathleen was in the car, motor running, doors locked.

Mac watched as JJ wandered through the rooms on the first floor. "How desperate for money were you? Was that why you fixated on the coins? On hunting me?"

"Who are you talking to, JJ?" Randy asked, two steps behind her. "I have money. See?"

He held his cloth wallet out to her. "I have $37 from my last paycheck. Do you want some?"

"No, but thank you." JJ smiled at her brother. "I was just talking to people who aren't here anymore."

"A dangerous habit to get into," Edgar said. "Do you think you could focus on finding those damn coins so we could get out of here. After our little trip to the woods, I'm not tolerating the cold as well as I did before. And this place is cold."

"Cold," Randy agreed. "Let's go home."

"First we need to find what we came for," Mac reminded them. "Randy, do you remember where Lisa Alvira hid Uncle Hugo's pirate coins? Can you show us?"

Randy rocked backed and forth on his heels.

"He's not ignoring you," JJ explained. "He's trying to put together an answer. This is hard for him."

"Come on kid, we don't have—"

JJ interrupted Edgar. "Just wait a minute."

Randy shrugged and made his way over to the staircase. "Maybe Roger didn't die. He might still be here."

"Is he talking about the bird again?" Jeff called out from the kitchen. "It's going to be dark in a couple of hours. If you don't hurry up, we'll have to get some lights brought in. Might attract the wrong kind of attention, if you know what I mean."

Randy started up the stairs. Mac, JJ, and Whiskey followed.

"JJ," Mac whispered, one hand on her arm as they stood outside a bedroom. "Are we wasting our time here? What's he—"

"This was my room," Randy announced. "All mine." He turned in a circle in the small bedroom, pointing out items that were no longer there. "My bed was there. My bookshelf was there. My chair was in that corner. Roger's cage was by the window. Roger has the coins."

Chapter 22

Mac walked over to the window in Randy's old room and stared out into the backyard. Late afternoon was quickly turning into evening. The best he could piece together from what Randy was telling them was that the gold coins had been in the bird cage. He wasn't sure how much credence he could give to the young man's recollection. And even if Randy was right, there certainly was no bird cage anywhere in sight now. He had a feeling Roger's cage was just as gone as Roger was. They were running out of time.

His back to the room, he listened to JJ try to coax more information from her brother.

"Aunt Lisa put the gold coins in Roger's cage? You saw her do that?"

"Uh huh. In a plastic baggie on the bottom of the cage with newspaper over the top so Roger's poo didn't get on them. She said Uncle Hugo would never find them there cause he didn't like to get his hands dirty. I wouldn't touch bird poo either. Aunt Lisa always took care of it, every morning."

"Mac?" JJ walked over to him. "The bird died some time during the last year that Randy and I lived here. I don't remember what happened to the cage. It was a big, old fashioned metal cage. I guess it's possible Lisa hid the coins in it."

"Do you think Doc Alvira ever saw the cage?" Mac glanced from JJ to Randy. "Would he have ever been in Randy's room?"

She shook her head. "I don't know. Probably not. It wasn't like he spent much time with us kids. Plus Aunt Lisa didn't like it when he showed up, she tried to keep us away from him. He was only here when he needed money. He and Uncle Hugo...they were brothers, but they hated each other. They did a few robberies together, but neither trusted the other."

"He killed Hugo over those coins. Kidnapped your brother to get them. Let's hope for Rachel's sake his greed makes him careless. We're going to have to give him what he wants, one way or another." Mac gestured towards the door. "Let's look through the rest of the house before it gets too dark. Then I think we'd better go shopping."

***

"What did Lieutenant Greeley say?" Edgar asked, putting a sandwich and cup of coffee in front of Mac.

They were in Edgar's kitchen. Mac had just spent twenty minutes getting his ass chewed out by his old boss and another half hour working out the details to a plan that he hoped wouldn't get anyone shot or killed before the night was over.

"To make a long story short and deleting the expletives, he's got Fiori and Giles over at the Smithsonian setting up surveillance teams. How are JJ and Kathleen doing on their project?"

"They're getting spray paint all over my garage. Cage might be a little tacky. Kathleen ran to the drugstore to get a hair dryer."

Mac shook his head. "Tacky doesn't matter. By the time Alvira gets his hands on it, we'll have Rachel back and the cops will have Alvira. Where's Randy?"

"Watching television in the den and going through my takeout menus. He's hungry again. I think he's got a hollow leg."

"Do you think you can get him to stay with you tonight? I'm not sure I can convince JJ to wait it out here, but I don't want to risk Randy being at the exchange. He's too unpredictable."

Edgar nodded. "Don't worry. I can handle him. By the time we get through a couple of pizzas and some tacos, you should all be back."

"I appreciate it. And what about that other thing?"

"I already called the old bat back. Told her you and Rachel were on a stakeout and Rachel would be back in the morning. Not sure she believed me."

Mac picked up the sandwich and took a bite. Swallowing, he said, "Rachel and her great aunt are close. Try to be nice if she shows up here."

Edgar chuckled. "I'm always nice."

***

"Can I talk to you for a few minutes?"

JJ wasn't sure this was the right time, but if something went wrong, it might be the only chance she would have to apologize.

Mac was standing in Edgar's kitchen, cup in hand, watching the coffeemaker fill a glass carafe. "I think Edgar owns the oldest *Mr. Coffee* still in existence. Or at least it's the slowest."

"I'm sorry." She sat down at the granite-topped kitchen island, putting her hands palm down on the cold surface. She stared at her hands. "Sorry about everything."

Mac leaned back against the counter opposite the island. "I don't understand why you didn't think you could trust me. I'm not sure I ever will."

She looked up for a moment, before lowering her gaze again. "I know. There's something missing in me. I don't...I can't trust people. I'm not going to make excuses for my behavior; but I don't think it's in me to change. It's never been anything you did or didn't do. I'm just sorry I got you involved in all this."

"Don't keep saying you're sorry," Mac said, filling his cup with the freshly made brew. "You need to figure out who you want to be. JJ Jarrett, the smart, creative, independent, young woman who never backed down from a challenge. Or Amanda Norman, the angry fourteen-year-old foster kid who started running and never stopped."

"I don't know." Her voice was barely a whisper.

"You think about it and we can talk more later. Right now I've got a job to do."

Mac took a last gulp of coffee and walked out.

Chapter 23

He didn't like it. Too many variables. Too much left to chance. And too damned cold.

Mac looked around. Initially Alvira and he had agreed to meet at midnight in front of the National Air and Space Museum, on the National Mall, the park that ran from the Washington Monument to the Capitol. Mac had worked with Lieutenant Greeley to have a SWAT team in the surrounding area. The plan was that they'd make the switch, gold for Rachel, and the professionals would move in.

But an hour earlier, he'd gotten a call from Alvira. Alvira sensing a trap had switched the location. The short call had ended with a plea from Rachel. "Don't bring the cops, Mac. He says if he smells a double-cross, he'll...." The call was ended abruptly.

So he was standing in a deserted playground in Arlington, Virginia, next to a rusted metal swing set which was missing two of the four swings. Under protest, Jeff and Kathleen had remained in the car, ready to call the cops if, or when, the bullets started flying. The only light was from a flickering street lamp.

Mac waited, wondering again if he was making a mistake, if his plan was too simple to work. But since he didn't have a better idea, he was stuck with this one.

He sensed rather than saw the two of them as they made their way through the snow-covered grass. Alvira was slightly behind

Rachel, undoubtedly his gun pointed at her back. No fast breaks for her.

"Where are the coins?"

Alvira's expression reminded Mac of a rattler in that instant before it strikes. The man stopped about five feet from where Mac stood.

The dim light caught the reflection of the metal barrel of the handgun.

Mac ignored the question. He needed to close the distance a little. Hoping Alvira wouldn't understand what he was doing, Mac stepped forward and reached out to lightly touch Rachel's hand. Her face was as pale as the snow on the ground. "You okay?"

She nodded, forcing a small smile. "Mr. Alvira and I are ready to part company."

"She said it! I'd forgotten how much trouble women are." He raised his gun, pointing it at Rachel's head. "I'm not going to ask you twice. The sound of bullets around here won't surprise anyone. First, lay your gun down on the ground and kick it towards me. I know you're packing so don't even try to deny it. And then I want the gold. You do it all nice and easy."

Mac reached into his shoulder holster and retrieved his gun. He dropped it and kicked it carefully the few feet towards Alvira.

Alvira maneuvered Rachel in front of the gun, then he leaned down and picked it up. He tucked it into his waistband.

While Alvira's attention and hand was on Mac's gun, Rachel stepped closer to Mac. She slipped her hands into her pockets.

"Where do you think you're going? Get back here."

She stood a little taller and turned to face Alvira. "Look. I've done what you wanted. You'll probably still kill us both, so give me a second with my boyfriend. I don't want to die without telling him...." Her voice broke.

Mac put his arms around Rachel and stepped back, increasing the distance between them and Alvira.

She turned and slumped against him, burying her face in his shoulder. He felt something slide into his right pocket.

"This is so touching." Alvira sneered, waving his gun at both of them. "If I could interrupt this little moment, I want my gold and I want it now."

Mac pushed Rachel behind him. He picked up a metal birdcage that had been sitting to one side on the ground.

Both Rachel and Alvira stared at it in confusion.

"Randy remembered. Lisa, Hugo's wife, hid the gold. JJ says she probably was trying to save enough to pay for a transplant, but then she got sicker, Hugo got arrested, you were already in jail...."

"Are you trying to tell me that Lisa had the gold melted and made into a damn birdcage?" Alvira pointed his gun at Mac. "I thought you understood that I'm done playing games. Is this a set-up?"

"No set-up. The gold is–"

"Stop talking!" Alvira glanced around wildly. "You called the cops didn't you?"

Mac moved backwards again, Rachel in lockstep with him.

"No, you fool. Lisa hid the gold in the bottom of the damn birdcage. Here take it." And with that statement, Mac swung the cage directly at Alvira's gun, pushing his arm to the side, and giving Mac the moment he needed to dive behind a snow-covered park bench, pulling Rachel to the ground with him.

"This better be a gun," Mac muttered, as he reached into his pocket and felt a familiar grip. "And it better be loaded."

"I wouldn't have risked giving it to you otherwise," Rachel mumbled, her face hidden in his jacket.

Alvira picked up the cage, fired his gun in the general direction of the couple, then started running towards his car, shooting off rounds as he went.

Mac returned fire, twice, stopping when he could no longer see Alvira. He heard a car engine and knew Alvira had fled the scene.

"Rachel, are you alright?"

Rachel nodded, sitting up and brushing off the snow. "If I'd known he was that bad a shot, I'd have walked away from him sooner."

Mac managed a chuckle, deciding not to tell her that he probably hadn't hit his target either. The good guys on television always hit what they were aiming at. In reality it wasn't that easy to shoot a fleeing bad guy in the dark.

Police sirens screamed through the night.

Mac got to his feet, holding out a hand to Rachel. "Let's get out of here."

The sound of a loud crash and the blaring of a car horn had them both flinching.

"What was that?" Rachel asked, holding his arm.

"Someone who has better aim than me and a bigger weapon." Mac suspected that Jeff's car was going to need some repair work.

But for the moment, Mac ignored the cold, the snow, and the endless sermon he was going to get from Lieutenant Greeley. For the one minute he had before all hell broke loose, he was going to hug his girlfriend.

Chapter 24

They were seated around her dining room table. He wasn't sure how he ended up at the head of the table, with Rachel at the other. It looked like one of those Norman Rockwell paintings. He smiled at the thought.

"Did you say something?" asked Jeff O'Herlihy, his wife Kathleen sitting next to him.

Mac shook his head.

He saw Jeff reach for another slice of pizza, then glance at Kathleen and grin.

"It's not sprouts, but there's nutrition in cheese."

Kathleen laughed and Mac saw his old friend smile even broader.

"Give me a slice of that pizza with pepperoni. I'll bike a little longer tomorrow." Kathleen winced. "Or maybe not."

"I can't believe you rammed that guy's SUV with my new Mercedes," Jeff said, pushing the pizza box closer.

"He was getting away." Kathleen checked her slice, then stole some extra pepperoni from the pie. "Sometimes you just have to grab the bull by the horns..." She took a bite and let out a sigh. "There is nothing like Luigi's pizza."

"You playing vigilante is gonna cost me a bundle," Jeff grumbled. "My car insurance rates will go up, mark my words."

Kathleen leaned over and gave her husband a kiss full on the lips. "Worth every penny. I wasn't going to let that scum escape."

"You're an adrenaline junkie," Jeff complained. "Admit it."

Kathleen kissed her husband again. "Maybe."

Mac laughed, surprising himself that he could find the dangerous situation funny in any way.

He looked at Rachel. Her hair was still wet from the shower, she had no make-up on, and yet he was struck by how beautiful she was. That thought was immediately followed by the realization that he was getting unbelievably sappy in his old age.

"Miz Brenner, you got any of those brownies left?" Edgar still had a nose cannula feeding him oxygen, but had color in his cheeks and apparently a healthy appetite.

Rachel laughed. "If you and Aunt Ella haven't finished them off."

She got up from her chair to bring some of her baked goods to the table.

"I haven't been snitching the brownies since I found out about this kidnapping business. Been too worried to eat a thing," Rachel's Great Aunt complained, although the tomato sauce on her chin seemed to betray her words.

"Then you're missing some mighty fine eatin'." Edgar took two garlic rolls from the bread basket.

Ella grabbed the now empty basket from the senior citizen, junior detective. "You might leave some for others."

"You snooze, you lose." Edgar cackled, but placed one of the rolls on Ella's plate, which she promptly picked up and finished in two bites.

"What happens next?" Rachel asked, placing a tray of assorted baked goodies in the middle of the table. She removed the almost empty pizza boxes, but first placed a slice on the empty paper plate in front of Whiskey. The dog woofed her appreciation.

All eyes turned to Mac. He wondered when he had become the fountain of wisdom.

"I think they'll be able to pin several murders on Alvira, multiple counts of kidnapping, burglary, arson, assorted Federal charges. Who knows if anyone will ever find those stolen gold coins. For my part I don't care if he gets Perry Mason to defend him, Alvira is going away for life."

"Good riddance."

Standing at the doorway was JJ Jarrett, his assistant formerly known as Amanda Norman. Once Mac and Rachel had returned and told her that Alvira had been arrested, JJ borrowed Rachel's car and took Randy back to the group home.

"I hope he fries."

Rachel motioned for JJ to sit next to her.

"Not likely," Mac said, "since DC doesn't have the death penalty. But he won't breathe air outside prison walls for the rest of his life."

"What kind of legal trouble am I in?" JJ asked quietly.

He was surprised when Ella stepped in. "I'm going to send you to an old friend of mine. Best lawyer in Virginia even if he's a tad too conservative about money matters for my tastes. He'll straighten out this mess."

"You don't know me." JJ cocked her head. "Why would you do that?"

Ella laughed. "Because that's what families and friends do for each other. Isn't that right, Rachel? Often they even stop them before they do something incredibly foolish."

She smiled at her niece.

Rachel nodded. "Are you going to stick around DC for awhile Aunt Ella?"

The older woman nodded. "Not DC so much. I'm going to Warrenton for a few weeks to visit friends, then back to sunny California, my fortune intact, thank you very much."

Rachel laughed.

"And if this old man would pass the plate of brownies, I might just eat one."

Edgar took another chocolate morsel, then handed the plate to Ella.

The group ate almost all the baked goods, but soon, exhaustion overtook all its members. Rachel packed up another container of leftovers for Edgar and JJ, who had decided to spend the night at the senior citizen's house.

"He needs someone to check on him," she whispered to Mac. "Tired as he is, the old fool is likely to forget to change out the oxygen canister before he goes to bed."

***

"I'll help you clean up," Mac offered. The house was quiet. It was just the two of them left.

Rachel laughed. "Thanks. But there's not much left to put away. Solving crimes apparently builds appetites." She stood at the sink, rinsing a few mugs before loading the dishwasher.

He stood behind, arms around her waist, head resting on her shoulder. "You're really quite something, Ms. Brenner."

He could feel her deep chuckle.

"You're pretty special yourself, Mr. Sullivan."

She turned off the faucet and turned to face him.

"For the first time, I really understand why they don't allow cops to investigate when their families are involved. It's impossible to be detached and professional when someone you...you..." Mac wasn't sure what verb to use and it scared him spitless.

Rachel smiled, brushed her hand across his cheek. "You did great. We're all safe, thanks to you."

Mac returned the smile and pulled her closer. "Thanks to this pistol-packing girlfriend I've got."

Rachel grinned. "You already asked me to go steady Mr. Sullivan. You did that at Thanksgiving. What are you after now?"

He knew what he wanted. He just wasn't sure she was in the same place in their relationship.

"I think I'm in love with you." He said the words without really intending to give voice to them.

The smile on her face disappeared, but she wrapped her arms around his neck.

He swallowed hard, hoping she'd say something.

She didn't.

The two held each others gaze for a long moment, then Mac leaned in for a kiss.

He might have gotten one too if Whiskey hadn't started nibbling on the cat's kibble.

A sharp hiss, an angry swipe, and the chase was on.

"Oh, for heaven's sake." Rachel started after the two animals, but Mac grabbed her hand and pulled her out of the kitchen. He firmly shut the door behind them.

"Let the children work it out for themselves."

"Okay." Rachel smiled. "I never got to show you that new dress I bought."

He nodded towards her staircase. "I'm free now. Do you want to—"

"Best idea you've had all week." She turned off the lights and started up the stairs. "You're going to love it."

He followed. He was sure he would.

The End

AUTHOR NOTES

Evelyn David is the pseudonym for Marian Edelman Borden and Rhonda Dossett. Marian lives in New York and is the author of twelve nonfiction books on a wide variety of topics ranging from veterans benefits to playgroups for toddlers! For more information on her books, please visit her website at:

www.marianedelmanborden.com

Rhonda lives in Muskogee, Oklahoma, is the director of the coal program for the state, and in her spare time enjoys imagining and writing funny, scary mysteries. Marian and Rhonda write their mystery series via the Internet. While many fans who attend mystery conventions have now chatted with both halves of Evelyn David, Marian and Rhonda have yet to meet in person.

Please check out Evelyn David's website and blog at:
http://www.evelyndavid.com
http://www.thestilettogang.blogspot.com/

BOOKS BY EVELYN DAVID

Sullivan Investigations Mystery Series
Murder Off the Books
Murder Takes the Cake
Murder Doubles Back
Riley Come Home - short story
Moonlighting at the Mall – short story

Sound Shore Times Mysteries
Zoned for Murder

Brianna Sullivan Mysteries
I Try Not to Drive Past Cemeteries
The Dog Days of Summer in Lottawatah
The Holiday Spirit(s) of Lottawatah
Undying Love in Lottawatah
A Haunting in Lottawatah
Lottawatah Twister
Missing in Lottawatah
Good Grief in Lottawatah
Summer Lightning in Lottawatah

Romance Stories
Love Lessons

Made in the USA
San Bernardino, CA
29 September 2013